THE YUKON WOLF

Brett Roehr

TABLE OF CONTENTS

Yukon Wolf

Family: Canidae

Genus: Canis

Species: Canis lupus

Subspecies: Canis lupus pambasileus

Average Height: 33 inches (84 cm) at the shoulder

Average Weight: 46 to 121 lbs. (21 to 55 kg)

Average Lifespan: 4 to 12 years

Range: Alaska, USA, and Yukon, Canada

Diet: Caribou, Dall sheep, moose etc.

The Characters

Arnaaluk's Family

Akiak – The uncle

Arnaaluk – The daughter

Kiviaq and Nova – Arnaaluk's brothers

Lusa – The aunt

Payuk – The father

Tulok's Family

Kanak – Tulok's jealous brother

Mammak – Tulok's father

Tulok – A lone wolf

Other Characters

Alasie – Lycargus' mate

Amak – Lycargus' brother

Lycargus – The villain

Chapter One

Anticipation

Today was her big day. Arnaaluk panted with anticipation about scoring her first caribou kill.

A howl broke the surrounding silence, interrupting her thoughts. Arnaaluk's eyes jerked open, rousing her from a daydream. She recognized it as the voice of her brother, Kiviaq. She paused, waiting for the next message. With the thrill of the upcoming hunt fresh on her mind, she wondered, *Is this it? Has the hunt begun?* Another howl came, the voice of validation. Yes, the hunt had begun.

She looked to the rocky peaks of the Ogilvie Mountains, northeast of the Yukon River. These were the grounds upon which her family had hunted for generations. She put her nose to the ground, scanning for caribou tracks and scent. Tracks littered the hills and forests before her. Taking in the scents of her surroundings, she singled out the one most important to her: caribou. In the dense forest, she gazed upon each of the spruce trees, observing the deep gashes cut in their trunks - gashes from the antlers of caribou and moose.

The skills she learned from her seniors throbbed in her bones: the value of strategy, skill, resourcefulness, and targeting the weakest in the herd. Now was the perfect time to test her skills in survival, to prove herself capable of living on her own.

Far ahead of the other wolves in pursuit, Arnaaluk kept her mind set on one thing - the prey. She wandered across the grassy valley, then stood still, listening for the hooves of caribou. At first, the air was silent, save for the evening wind rustling through the tall grass and trees. A strong caribou scent touched her nostrils. As she sniffed the air for confirmation, a shiver ran down her back and saliva filled her mouth. A howl came to her throat, calling the wolves to follow her.

Arnaaluk kept her eyes focused, each track a sign pointing her ahead. She ran her tongue across her teeth, her body trembled and her heart raced with impatience.

Despite her skill, thoughts of doubt and fear of failure flooded her mind. She could almost taste the warm flesh of caribou in her mouth and see her father's stance as he acknowledged her kill. Another thought entered her mind unbidden - sharp antlers and hooves. The vision of her own broken form, trampled, gored or kicked.

Despite these fears, she was determined. Now was the chance to make her first kill, an opportunity she could not resist. Deep in a nearby valley she paused. Before her was a spot where the scent of caribou was the strongest. She rolled in it, slathering it over her body.

With her mind cleared, she stood in silence. She pointed her ears forward, heeding the audible rhythm of hooves from afar. Climbing to the hilltop overlooking a valley, she gazed upon a large herd grazing below.

For a moment, she caught her breath. "This is it! The prey is mine at last!"

Arnaaluk stared at the herd, studying each individual caribou. She waited for the other wolves to catch up with her, but one caribou caught sight of their approach. A wave of fear spread through the herd as they stared back at the wolves. Flocks of hungry ravens gathered overhead, watching as spectators, waiting for their chance to partake of a great feast of venison.

As soon as she was close enough, Arnaaluk crouched in the tall grass, anticipating the moment she would take down her first caribou. Determination overwhelmed her and her heart pounded. She took one small step, then another. With every step she used caution, knowing one sudden move could scare away the prey. Now was her time to mature and discover the true nature of the wolf. Once close enough she paused, waiting for the prey to make the first move, for one foolish caribou to turn and run.

Arnaaluk had one choice. Take the next step. Chase the prey and make a kill.

Chapter Two

In for the Kill

Before long, the silence was broken. Thundering hooves echoed through the valley. The wolves picked up speed, dashing after the panicked herd. First came the weaker wolves to lead the chase, to test the prey: Arnaaluk's brothers, Kiviaq and Nova, along with her aunt Lusa. Then came the stronger wolves: Arnaaluk, her father Payuk, and her uncle Akiak, trailing from behind to make the kill.

Kiviaq rushed after the herd, shifting his eyes back and forth. He sought the most vulnerable - the elderly, the young, the crippled, or the sick. Braving the torrent of hooves stampeding around him, he wedged himself between an adolescent bull he had singled out, and the rest of the herd. It was a strategic move aimed at breaking up the herd and weakening their natural defenses.

Kiviaq nipped at the hindquarters. The caribou kicked at him with his sharp, powerful hooves, but each kick swished over Kiviaq. With one leap, he nipped at the hindquarters in midair, but missed on the first try. He jumped forward a second time, catching the caribou's flank. Trying to maintain his grip, he endured the caribou's struggle, every buck and kick. He glanced behind to find Arnaaluk catching up with him, but the powerful blow of a caribou hoof struck Kiviaq in the cheek. Not losing his grip, he sheared away a small chunk of fur and hide with his strong teeth. It was enough to create a small wound.

With her greatest opportunity looming before her, Arnaaluk focused on the caribou's throat. Just then, she noticed the caribou kicking Kiviaq away, so Arnaaluk shifted her focus to the hindquarters. She chomped at the flank, removing a large ball of fur, but no hide and flesh. Jumping forward and nipping again, she tore open a deeper wound. Arnaaluk was panting and nearly out of breath, but she pressed on. She could not give up.

Being weakened by vast amounts of blood spewing from his hindquarters, the caribou slowed to a canter. Arnaaluk seized him with her teeth once more, working to inflict the deepest wound possible. She yelped in pain after a sharp kick to her shoulder and was jolted for a moment, but this would be the caribou's last triumph.

Sapped from loss of blood, the caribou finally collapsed. Arnaaluk ran to his head and clamped onto his throat with her jaws. The caribou struggled, then toppled to its side. She tightened her grip and heard the caribou's last bleats of agony.

The other wolves mobbed the caribou. With the trauma inflicted upon it, the caribou took its last breath. The ravens swarmed on the kill. They landed eagerly upon the carcass, struggling between the wolves for their share.

First to eat, Akiak and Lusa gnawed on the carcass. They tore off lumps of fur and chewed on the hide. Placing his front paws on the caribou's back, Payuk snarled at his son Kiviaq, warning him to stay away as the elder wolves ate their fill. With the fur on his back raised, he warned his pups to wait, asserting his parental dominance over them.

Kiviaq took one sniff of the carcass, but Payuk nipped him as a stern warning. Then Nova crept toward the carcass, crouching before Payuk and was granted permission to eat. Payuk turned his head toward Arnaaluk and glared at her, and in obedience, she released the throat. When Kiviaq approached the carcass a second time, Payuk gave him one strong nip on the shoulder. He yelped and whimpered in pain, backing away before the supremacy of his father.

"Wait your turn!" Payuk growled.

Payuk would not allow Arnaaluk and Kiviaq to take one bite of the carcass until Nova had eaten his fair share. For Payuk, each snarl and growl were a warning, each nip was an act of discipline. Payuk knew that Kiviaq would devour more than his share of the meat at the kill site. As a result, his brother would not have enough to eat.

Finally, Payuk turned his head away from Kiviaq, granting him access to the carcass. He glared at Arnaaluk for a few moments to give Kiviaq time to eat, then moved out of the way. Soon, both raven and wolf demolished the carcass together, devouring all they could eat.

For Payuk, the caribou kill was a welcome sight. This caribou was part of a herd he'd been tracking for three days. As the father, Payuk was the curator of the family's knowledge regarding caribou - their migration routes, and the skills required to hunt them. This made him important to their survival. Having witnessed the caribou kill Arnaaluk had accomplished, he gave her a lick to her muzzle. It was a job well done. All the time he had spent training her to hunt had paid off.

It was now late summer and caribou were abundant this season. Payuk had lived through seasons of starvation and seasons of plenty. He watched the sunset descend over the hills on the west side of the river. Another day had passed and a harsh winter was on its way.

Chapter Three

Arnaaluk and Her Brothers

Once the other wolves had eaten and settled to rest, Arnaaluk rolled in the grass, celebrating her first caribou kill. She climbed to a ledge on a nearby mountainside overlooking the other wolves. Resting under the twilight sky, the cool breeze resonated on her black fur. Howling in victory from her lofty position, she proclaimed her first kill to her family, and to every creature in range. Now she could prove herself a worthy hunter to the other wolves in the family.

For Arnaaluk, there was a time to hunt and a time to rest. The time to rest was always an opportunity to practice skills in hunting prey. To her, spruce cones resembled voles, a large stone resembled a snowshoe hare, while the other wolves in her family were as caribou. A wolf her size matched that of a growing caribou calf. Scuffling and fighting with her siblings built up her strength, and everything she could pick up with her teeth was a toy. With these tools, she could hone her skills to become an ideal hunter.

Life was not always easy for her. As a pup, she had watched the runt of her littermates starve to death during their first winter. For much of her early life, Arnaaluk had dominated her siblings in fights over meat and bones so she rarely went hungry. She was spoiled and well-fed. Her mother, Alatna, had fallen ill and died the past winter. For a time, Arnaaluk was lost in grief, unable to bear the loss.

Arnaaluk picked up a spruce cone. She held it in her jaws and tossed it in the air, catching it upon descent. She nudged it with her nose, watching it roll across the ground and then batted it with her paw. The spruce cone flew over the ledge and tumbled down the mountainside, bouncing across the rocks and through the grass. Arnaaluk picked up another spruce cone and crushed it with her teeth. She thought of it as a vole being crushed by her jaws.

Arnaaluk looked on the other wolves in her family with great affection. With fond memories of her play-fighting and scuffling with them, she gazed upon her brothers as they slept. Arnaaluk's love for her brothers was deep and unconditional.

A thought crossed her mind. She needed to sharpen her skills in tackling and killing prey. Who better to practice this with than her two siblings?

Kiviaq's howl interrupted her thoughts. From the tone of his voice, she recognized an invitation to play. She jumped and dashed toward him. As her tail wagged with excitement, she picked up a spruce branch and scurried down the mountainside.

For Kiviaq, life on the lower end of sibling rivalry was sometimes difficult. On some days, it meant hunger. Other times, it meant being nipped for disobeying the rules of his big sister. Sometimes, it meant living on bare bones. He would often approach Arnaaluk with his tail tucked between his legs, his shoulders hunched, and his head lowered out of respect.

Kiviaq desired to leave home and find a mate of his own who was a great hunter, much like his sister. However, he still felt uneasy about leaving the family. Like his big sister, he possessed an emotional connection to his family, without which he could not survive. Starvation had always been his greatest fear, and even in adulthood, the memory of losing his smallest and youngest sibling to starvation haunted him. Because he had not yet sharpened his hunting skills, he knew he wasn't ready to leave.

Kiviaq pranced about as he watched his sister approach. "What have you been doing on this fine night?" he asked.

"I was sitting on that ledge...enjoying the gorgeous landscape," she replied.

Kiviaq grasped her branch with his jaws. "How's the weather up there?"

"It's nice!" She nudged him, tipping him until he fell on his side. She lay on him, pinning him to the ground. "I hear the air pressure is dropping!"

Kiviaq struggled under her weight. "You're very strong!"

"Strong enough to take down a caribou larger than you!"

A nip on the tail jolted her. Arnaaluk turned to find her other brother, Nova. He stood behind her, panting mischievously, then turned and ran. Arnaaluk, releasing her hold on Kiviaq, chased him, tackling and then giving him a strong bite to the shoulder. He yelped and backed away.

Arnaaluk paused. "I'm sorry, I didn't mean to bite you so hard." She kissed Nova on the side of the muzzle.

"It's fine, I'm all right!" whispered Nova.

Arnaaluk knew her limitations and the rules of play. She was careful not to be too rough with her siblings or they would avoid her. Her displays of dominance would never exceed the level of her father. "I know the rules," she said, "If you want to enjoy scuffling with others, you must earn their trust."

As she finished saying this, Kiviaq trotted away from her, holding her branch in his mouth. In retaliation for his theft, she rushed toward him and seized his neck with her teeth, toppling him a second time. She pulled him across the ground by the scruff of his neck, until his jaws lost their grip on the branch. She placed her paws on his back and shoulders.

She looked down at him, staring him in the face. "I can't describe how excited I am to have taken down a caribou for the first time!"

Kiviaq struggled, but Arnaaluk restrained him, pretending he was a small caribou. "Not so fast! For now, you are still my prey!"

Kiviaq lay with his teeth bared in submission to her. "Are you going to give me the fatal bite?"

"Why would I do that? We're just playing!"

Despite her status as the big sister, Arnaaluk loved her two brothers and they were almost inseparable. Together, they hunted, played, rested, and howled, and together they had grieved the loss of their mother.

Arnaaluk had dominated Kiviaq, but both she and Kiviaq dominated Nova, the lowest of the siblings. Nova would often cower before her, flipping over on his back. Whenever she played tag with him, he was often the victim.

Once she finished scuffling with her brothers, Arnaaluk yawned, resting her haunches in the grass. As she looked at the rising sun following the short summer night, Kiviaq huddled next to her. The two wolves gazed on the stunning panorama. Closeness beamed over them like the warmth of the sun's rays on a cool morning.

In spite of her family ties, Arnaaluk focused on what lay ahead. She gazed upon the mountains to the north, aching with a different type of loneliness. It was central to every wolf to seek a mate. She knew life was more than simply catching prey, it was also having a family of her own.

She also knew, however, the warnings of her father - not to venture outside their territory where danger lurked. Danger from other wolves, from bears and moose, danger from traps and guns. For her safety, she felt compelled to stay within the family borders. For a time, though, she listened for a howl from another wolf, but no wolf was heard. She closed her eyes and sighed, then faded off to sleep.

Payuk perched on a mound overlooking the open landscape, his mind plagued with responsibility regarding his offspring. His age reflected in the pain of his arthritic bones. He remembered when he and his brother and sister settled in the woodlands along the river, and when he met his future mate,

Alatna. Over the years, they had many litters of pups and forged a life together.

From time to time, Payuk had returned to the land of his birth and met with his old family. After the birth of his second litter, he met his parents for the last time. Over time, his old family had gradually traveled north, and soon, they were far away. He did not remember the last time he heard their howls. He thought less and less about them and moved on with his routine, raising pups and maintaining a close bond with his new family.

For their last litter, they were unable to find a den so he and Alatna raised their pups on the forest floor. That is where Arnaaluk and her siblings were born with little shelter from the rain or snow. Arnaaluk, the first-born black pup of the litter, was born early one rainy summer. Payuk thought back on the times he spent with her, the times she had been a playful young pup, frolicking through the grass and snow. He remembered the first winter he spent with his last litter, when the runt died from starvation.

In time, Alatna became ill and died. Payuk was left with two siblings, two sons, and a daughter. He contemplated how his daughter, Arnaaluk, had changed after Alatna's death. As time passed, she grew into a troublesome, spoiled adolescent.

Since the death of his mate, it had been a time of trouble, grief, and loneliness and now bitterness filled Payuk's heart. Alatna had held a place in his heart no other wolf could fill, and his life seemed futile. From the time Payuk first courted her, they developed a strong bond, but now she was gone and the bond was broken forever. Finding a new mate was impossible for him. A mate is almost always irreplaceable for a wolf, especially for one beyond his prime.

Payuk's sister, Lusa, sat beside him, placing her paw on his shoulder. "You should be very proud of your daughter. I am impressed with her skills in hunting."

"You are the closest thing she has to a mother," Payuk uttered, "You've raised no pups of your own."

Lusa looked upon Arnaaluk and her brothers with tender feelings as they slept. "I raised them and nursed them while their mother was away. They were my pups, too. I didn't give birth to them, but I felt an instinct come over me from time to time. You know, the feeling you get when you're about to bear offspring of your own."

"Yes," Payuk recalled, "I remember, and you've cared for them ever since."

"She and her brothers still need a mother."

Payuk, resisting the thought of finding another mate, growled at her. "I'm getting too old to find another mate. They're getting too old to have a mother. They've almost matured. Ever since Alatna died, Arnaaluk has been troublesome..."

Lusa interrupted. "She's still learning about the true nature of the wolf. Now is not the time to lose faith in the younger generation. She must learn to hunt and establish strong bonds with others. She must learn to face her fears and survive."

Payuk sighed and shook his head as he descended the mound and rested in the soft grass. As he closed his weary eyes, he watched Lusa approach Arnaaluk, kissing her on the head, then rubbing her face against her neck to wish her a good rest.

Chapter Four

A Quest for Independence

A searching howl sounded across the valley. This time, not a call to a hunt, but the howl of a stranger, perhaps a lone wolf. Arnaaluk awoke and yawned. She stretched her legs and perked her ears. Dashing down the hillside, she paused briefly to look back upon the other wolves. All were fast asleep, including Payuk. She continued on her way, racing through the valley.

She scanned and sniffed the grass, searching for the scent of marked territory. Cautiously, she trotted up the hillside. On the summit, a single wolf wandered, but paused to howl from time to time. She crept toward him, but the wolf caught sight of her and curled his lips. She froze and crouched before him, baring her teeth in submission, pleading with him to refrain from attack. She sniffed him on the neck. By his scent, she recognized him as part of a familiar bloodline that once lived in this area. The two wolves ran circles around each other.

"Hello! What are you doing here? My name is Kanak. You must be from those wolves living along the river."

Arnaaluk watched the stranger as he sniffed and licked her shoulders and side. She jumped away from him, startled by his sudden advances.

"My name is Arnaaluk. Are you from those wolves living to the north? Beyond the great mountains?" she stammered in a timid voice.

"I was… I broke with them two winters ago."

Arnaaluk took a deep breath. "That's interesting. I used to hear their howls all the time while I was growing up. My father told me stories about them. They hunted caribou, didn't they?"

"We did. Do you wish to know the story of my life? I was born in a den, at the foot of a great mountain, one you can barely see from here…"

Arnaaluk was curious about his courage. "Can you fight like a wolf?" she interrupted, "That's the quality I admire in a male."

"Yes…I may not be the dominant sibling of the litter, but I know how to fight!"

"Are you a great hunter?" she asked.

Kanak hesitated to answer. "Are caribou difficult for you to catch?"

Arnaaluk sighed. "Kind of difficult. Catching and killing caribou is a skill you master. I recently killed my first caribou."

"Great!" Kanak exclaimed, "Let's stay together."

Arnaaluk turned her back to him. "Sorry…I just don't know you."

Payuk's howl interrupted their brief encounter. Kanak turned his head in its direction. "I think I hear someone calling your name. Your father perhaps?"

Arnaaluk looked upon Kanak with intrigue about his background. Although she didn't know much about him, she

16

was desperate for a mate. To Arnaaluk, it was an exit strategy from a life of domination by her father.

Arnaaluk gave Kanak a lick to the nose. "Stick around these parts and howl for me later. I've got other things to do."

"Like what?"

"Oh, just… things! Tracking caribou."

Kanak understood. "Very well, then."

Mesmerized by her beautiful appearance, Kanak gazed upon Arnaaluk as she departed. He followed her downhill from a distance. With his sights on the young black wolf, he lowered his nose to the ground, sniffing her tracks in the damp mud. He followed her trail to the edge of the nearby valley, next to the woodlands by the river. From a distance, he saw her approach the other wolves in the small family unit. He could see only six of them.

Kanak wanted to learn more about this young wolf and those close to her. Hoping his search for a mate would end here, he would observe them from a safe distance. He spied on them cautiously, sniffing the ground for marked territory. He was aware her father could kill an intruder.

As a pup, Kanak had lived a life of privilege, much like Arnaaluk. Born into a litter of seven, he fought all his siblings over meat and bone and won. At first, he had never known about being a subordinate brother until his brother toppled him in a fight. Now, having escaped his brother's dominance, he was ready to find a mate for himself and raise a family. For now, there was no brother to keep him in line. Kanak stood atop the nearby hill for the rest of the morning and into the afternoon. He hoped Arnaaluk would be back soon and wanted to keep her within range.

Earlier that morning, Payuk awoke from his sleep. He howled, summoning the wolves to track more prey. He looked down the hillside where Kiviaq and Nova slept. Kiviaq and Nova were there, but Arnaaluk was gone. He descended the hill and stood in the midst of the valley, howling for her.

He looked in every direction, searching for his daughter. "Arnaaluk! What happened to her? Where could she be?"

He turned his head toward the east. There she was, approaching him from behind.

"At last! There you are! Where have you been? And what have you been doing?"

"I was out tracking caribou!" Arnaaluk sniffed her own fur, then gasped. She tried to back away from him.

Payuk sniffed the same spot on her fur. He found the scent of a strange wolf. His face filled with rage and fear. "You've been wandering outside our territory, haven't you?"

Arnaaluk snarled back in rebellion. "I was tracking caribou. This wolf approached and sniffed me. That's all that happened. Now leave me alone! I can go wherever I want! I'm now an adult!"

Infuriated by her rebellion, Payuk nipped her on the backside. He nudged her over, pinning her to the ground. "You've lied to me! You were not tracking caribou! I've told you countless times to stay in our territory and away from strange wolves. Why don't you listen?"

He placed his teeth near the veins in her neck. "I will let you off with a warning! Don't lie to me again, and don't leave our territory! This is important! I don't want you torn to shreds. Is that understood? This is for your safety."

"Enough!" she snapped, "I've had enough of you! I'm not a pup anymore! Stop treating me like one!"

"I don't care how old you are," Payuk growled, "I'm your father and you will obey me!" He released her.

Rising to her feet, Arnaaluk sighed and covered her nose with her paw, standing helpless before her father. Payuk circled her, keeping her under constant surveillance. She trembled, yearning for her father to recognize and respect her maturity.

Arnaaluk sulked in the grass, as her father sniffed the woods for signs of prey. Kiviaq crept up on her and playfully nipped her on the scruff of her neck.

Arnaaluk nudged him away. "I want to be left alone!" she mumbled. She climbed up to a rocky ledge overlooking the mountains.

"What's wrong?" asked Kiviaq.

19

"Never mind what's wrong," she growled, "It's none of your business. Just go away! Don't you have anything else to do?"

A howl from Payuk summoned them. Kiviaq followed the howl, then turned his head toward her. "Come on! Let's find more prey!"

Slumped over from loneliness and her recent correction, Arnaaluk was exasperated. She sighed and rolled her eyes. She followed Kiviaq and the others as they trotted north in search of caribou.

Arnaaluk forgot about the caribou. She was not hungry. She kept her mind focused on the lone wolf she encountered that morning. She wondered what became of his family, a family of wolves she had not seen or heard in two winters. As the other wolves stopped to rest, she sulked by herself along the banks of the river. With her ears listening for a howl, she sat daydreaming about him.

Payuk approached her. She lay silent before him. Her heart ached with the stare of her father's disapproval.

Payuk let out a sigh. "I don't think you're mature enough to survive on your own. If you think I'm too harsh with you, wait until you're living by yourself. Wait until you're facing starvation and the elements. Just think! In your whole lifetime, you have only caught one caribou. Not on your own, but with some help. That was yesterday. You still have a lot to learn, and you still need more time."

Arnaaluk did not respond. She kept her head turned away, ignoring him. Payuk stood there silent, watching her. After some time, he left her alone.

Arnaaluk struggled with indecision. In her heart, she was determined to hunt large prey by herself, but she was aware of her lack of experience. For now, she had to stay with her family to develop her hunting skills and provide for them. Mostly, however, she cared about her independence. Nothing else mattered as much.

As she lay along the riverside, a howl caught her ears. She recognized the voice of Kanak calling her name. For a moment, she thought of howling back, then raised her head and pointed it north. Hesitation gripped her, and the howl remained trapped in her throat. Confined by the threats of her father, her head sank to the ground.

Then, another howl caught her ear. It was a different voice coming from another wolf. The strange howl was soon joined by that of Kanak. These two howled as if they knew each other!

The other wolves ignored the two howls, all except for Kiviaq. Suspecting two strangers were watching them, he turned to Payuk.

"Two strangers! They're approaching our territory! Should we howl back?"

Payuk nudged him away. "No! Those wolves aren't doing anything suspicious."

Kiviaq sniffed a patch at the edge of the trees. "They've marked their territory right here. Are they…"

"Kiviaq! Ignore those two wolves. We've got to keep going!"

Kiviaq tried to run up the hillside, but Payuk stood in his way. "Do as you're told! Those two strangers are the least of our worries for now. I am your father and you will obey me!"

The young wolf crouched before him. "Yes! I...will do as you say."

Payuk looked ahead to find his two siblings Akiak and Lusa far ahead of him. He knew they were on the trail of caribou. Hearing a howl coming from Lusa, Payuk looked behind to find Arnaaluk sniffing the ground. Assuming she would not slip away, he continued farther north. He found a caribou track in the mud along the river, and the scent of fresh caribou filled his lungs. For the moment, he forgot about his daughter.

Arnaaluk watched the other wolves until they were out of sight. With Payuk distracted, a strong temptation overcame her. She knew the right thing to do was to track caribou with them, but an urge pulled her away. She could not control herself, and in spite of her father's warning, she sneaked away. She would suffer the consequences, but her greatest desire was to find a mate of her own. For now, that was all she cared about.

She took one last look at the other wolves. "I'm sorry... I must go."

Arnaaluk disappeared over the nearby hill. She sniffed the air, listened and scurried toward the mountains in the north.

Another sound caught her attention - the calls of a flock of ravens. They appeared on the horizon, circling overhead.

Arnaaluk followed them to the foot of the hill, the site where she and the other wolves camped the night before.

When the howl sounded again, she ran forward, looking for its source. Near the summit, she stopped to catch her breath. A set of tracks belonging to another wolf appeared before her. By their scent, she knew it was Kanak, that same lone wolf she had met that morning. He was also tracking prey. She trotted straight to the summit of the hill.

Chapter Five

Lycargus

A familiar wolf appeared before her eyes. He stood gazing upon the flocks of ravens above. Arnaaluk ran toward him and sniffed his fur, this time without apprehension.

Kanak turned to sniff her back. "Hello! Good to see you again! See those ravens in the sky?"

The ravens meant caribou were not far away.

Arnaaluk jumped with excitement. "Yes, I see them. Wherever the ravens gather, there a carcass will be. In times of starvation, they are your guides. That's what my father taught me."

Kanak nudged her, then turned his head to the flock. "Follow me!"

Arnaaluk tailed him and the ravens downhill into a nearby forest. She looked up to find the noisy birds perched in a tree.

Kanak ascended the mountainside, sniffing for signs of caribou or a carcass. He turned his head to her and panted. Arnaaluk, by contrast, felt uneasy about her surroundings. She sniffed the markings of a wolf on a fallen tree. The scent was familiar, and dread overcame her. She was now in the territory of a dreaded rival family of wolves. A family of large and robust moose hunters. These ravens were not after wolves stalking caribou, but moose! She had only one choice - turn and run!

Arnaaluk dashed toward Kanak. She tugged him by the scruff.

"What's the matter?" asked Kanak.

"We must get out of here! It's Lycargus!"

Upon the mention of his name, Kanak froze for a moment, then turned and ran. Just as Arnaaluk prepared to flee, she picked up the sound of footsteps approaching. Emerging from among the trees was a large, bulky wolf. His face was familiar to her, a face her father had taught her to dread. She froze and crouched in fear before him - Lycargus. Lycargus curled his lips at the intruder. He raised the fur on his back and pointed his tail in a horizontal position, the signal to attack.

"An intruder! Looks like someone was unlucky enough to stumble into my domain."

Arnaaluk snarled back. The fur on her shoulders stood on end, but it was no use. Her appearance could not intimidate him. She knew no wolf could frighten Lycargus. Even a larger animal such as a moose, was powerless before him.

He sniffed her fur, then placed his teeth next to her neck. "I recognize that scent!" he rasped, "The offspring of my most hated enemy, Payuk!"

Arnaaluk knew this was the end. She could not turn around and run from him. She had made a fatal mistake – intruding into the territory of other wolves, something her father had warned her of. Now, she would reap the consequences of disobedience. She closed her eyes, hoping this was a nightmare, but it was futile. She could not awaken from it. This was real.

Just then, she felt another wolf nudging her from behind. She glanced quickly and there stood a large wolf. It was another lone wolf, perhaps the one whose howl she heard earlier that day. He was big and bulky with a tenacious attitude. His tawny brown, gold, and beige fur was covered with scars. Nudging her out of the way, he came between her and Lycargus, and glared into the face of Lycargus with his golden eyes and curled his lips.

Arnaaluk watched the two wolves glaring at each other. She whirled around and sneaked away, hoping to avoid the carnage about to unfold. She began to run until she reached a safe distance outside marked territory.

"Tulok!" Lycargus whispered, "You are bold! Didn't I tell you not to come over here and flirt with my daughters? I almost killed you twice! I thought you'd learned your lesson."

Tulok raised the fur on his back. "I don't take lessons from you."

"May I ask why you were bold enough to confront me on behalf of that intruder? Do you know her personally?"

"No!" he answered.

"Then why are you trying to be a hero?"

"I am trying to do the right thing."

"Trying to do the right thing? Well, it looks like you've made a foolish mistake," he sneered. "You've already gotten away from me twice, but you won't this time. Any last words?"

"No! I don't have any last words for you."

The fight began. Lycargus lunged at Tulok. He seized him by the neck with his jaws and threw him to the ground. Tulok pulled away from him, but the grip of Lycargus' teeth tore off a piece of his fur. Tulok fought back, mauling Lycargus on the shoulder. Lycargus yelped in pain then jumped back at him. He ripped another chunk of fur from Tulok's shoulder.

Tulok knew the size and strength of Lycargus. Even though Tulok was taller, Lycargus was more muscular. To Tulok, he was almost as powerful as a bear. Fighting him off or tackling him was futile for a weaker wolf. Tulok was also aware the commotion might summon the other wolves. He turned and ran, realizing now was not a good time to be a hero and sacrifice his life. He rushed through the trees with Lycargus on his tail.

Lycargus chased Tulok downhill. As he descended the steep crag, Lycargus slipped. He tumbled down the mountainside, landing in a pile of hard icy snow. Following his humiliating spill, Lycargus jumped back to his feet and paused to catch his breath, but Tulok had disappeared. Because of his superior speed, he had vanished over the nearby hill and out of sight.

Chapter Six

A Brotherly Reunion

All clear! Tulok sighed with relief. He rested on the forest floor, pondering the mysterious female he had just encountered. He sniffed the ground until he found her scent and tracks in the damp mud. As he searched through the woods, he avoided the territory of Lycargus.

Suddenly, as he searched, he saw the flash of an unfamiliar wolf in the trees. Tulok stared warily as the other wolf approached and sniffed him. He snarled, expecting him to be part of Lycargus' family, but as he looked into the wolf's eyes, he noticed something familiar. These were not the eyes of a stranger, but the eyes of someone he had grown up with, a member of his own family. Tulok paused to sniff his fur. It was his younger brother, Kanak, the one he had dominated during his early life.

Tulok rolled Kanak over on his back, placing his paws on his chest. "Good to see you alive and well, Kanak. I haven't picked up your scent since the day you left home. I knew from your howl you were somewhere around here." He circled and scowled at him. "From the time you left our family, I never wanted to see you again, Kanak!" He released him, then nipped him on the shoulder, warning him to back off.

"Tulok!" Kanak exclaimed, "This is no way to treat your brother!"

"You were not just a brother. You were a bully and a nuisance! When we were pups, you devoured most of our food.

28

You left me living off bare bones until I was hardly alive! I have never forgiven you for it! I was happy the day I finally beat you in a fight!"

"That's the price of dominance," Kanak replied, "Only the strong will survive."

"Yes, spoken like a formerly dominant brother."

To their parents and siblings, Kanak and Tulok had always been known as "the two feuding brothers." Over time, Tulok would emerge as the victor in this rivalry. Tulok was easily triggered to anger and lost his temper every time his brother would challenge his authority. Through intimidation, Tulok kept Kanak in line and frequently used him as an outlet for his rage. For Tulok, nothing would ever come between him and his food, especially Kanak.

Tulok felt a stab of remorse. He dropped his head and tail to the ground. He trotted to the edge of the forest by a stream. "I'm sorry about how I treated you."

"Sorry?" Kanak grumbled, "You should be!" He rubbed his head against Tulok's neck. "I realize you've had a tough life. I only wish I could spend one more day with our brothers, sisters and parents, but now that you and I are together, it's time to forget the past. We're together again, and that's all that matters. I wandered around these hills along the great river, thinking of you, and our family long gone. I haven't heard from them in ages. Not one howl."

Tulok paused, sighed, then turned around. "I guess you're the closest thing I have to family now."

Kanak licked Tulok on the muzzle, determined to reconnect with his brother. They walked shoulder to shoulder, wagging their tails.

"Can you tell me everything that's happened since you've been gone?" asked Kanak.

"I'll talk about it later, it's a long and boring story. Now is probably not the time."

"Have you found a mate yet?"

"No, but I'm sure you've probably found one."

"Yes, Arnaaluk! I guess I'd better…"

"Go look for her?" Tulok interrupted, "I noticed you ran away when her life was in danger. She's probably not happy with you about that."

"Well, it was good to see you again. Be sure to keep in touch, Tulok. I hope you can catch caribou like our father."

"I can, I've killed some caribou on my own. Just watch me next time."

On the day Kanak broke with the family, Tulok was happy to see him leave. He had wished for a happy life with his parents and siblings, but this was all cut short by tragedy. Now Tulok was alone, but he and Kanak shared a similar plight. They had wandered the mountains and forests along the great river, in search of a mate to call their own. For Tulok, it had been an uneasy reunion.

Tulok sadly watched his brother trot away. "Maybe it's better if we don't stay together," he muttered.

As soon as he was gone, Tulok stood in the clearing. He picked up a large moose antler lying on the ground, carried it about, then tossed it a great distance. Lonely and bored, he yawned, resting his chin in a patch of old snow. The young wolf sighed with frustration. He knew life as a recluse was not natural for a wolf, and to function in the wild, he must be part of a family unit. It was clear. He hated living this way. He desired to be social and connect with others, but most importantly, to find a mate.

Chapter Seven

Released!

Arnaaluk stood on the nearby hill overlooking the river. She was ready to rejoin her father and face whatever consequences awaited her, if any. Her heart was racing, and her nerves were tingling in dread of what could happen once she got back. As she stood on the hill, Kanak approached her. Arnaaluk, disgusted with his act of cowardice before Lycargus, turned her back to him.

She swatted him across the face with her tail. "You lack bravery and willingness to fight! You fled when my life was in danger! I deserve someone better than you!"

"Like who?" he asked.

"Someone else!" she snapped.

The experience of nearly being torn to shreds by Lycargus was still fresh on her mind. Although she longed to be back with her family, she was afraid of her father's reaction.

Kanak pleaded with her. "Now wait just a moment…"

Arnaaluk turned her head to take one last look at him. "No! I'm finished talking with you, I've got to get back to my family. I hope they didn't notice I was gone!"

With her chest puffed out and an angry sigh, Arnaaluk ascended the hillside, disappearing over the summit.

At last, she reached the edge of the river and found the area where she last saw her father and the other wolves tracking caribou, but they were gone. Arnaaluk was nervous. She traveled north of the river where she found their scent, and crossed a nearby hill where she found them resting in a valley. Her father was waiting for her.

"Where have you been?" demanded Payuk.

Arnaaluk halted in her tracks and cowered before him in submission. Her ears burned with fear.

Payuk approached her and sniffed her fur. "Why won't you answer me?"

"I wandered away," she said, "What do you want from me? I deserve better things than merely providing for you and the family!"

Her brother, Kiviaq, interjected. "No! Don't say that!"

Payuk nipped her on the shoulder. He pressed her to the ground, holding her for a few moments. "You know what this means," he warned. "You want to live a life of your own. I understand that, but I fear for your safety!"

Arnaaluk shivered as he towered over her.

Payuk sighed heavily. "I can tell you desire a mate. I understand you can't stay with us forever, and I am approaching the end of my life. Most of your siblings are gone. They have left home to seek their own way in this world. As for you, you're free to be on your own. You will follow the instinct of every other wolf. The time has come! Now you must leave home!"

As each moment passed, Arnaaluk realized her foolishness. Her disobedience had brought her to the point of no return. This would be a day she would never forget - the day her father released her into the unknown, into a world full of dangers.

Payuk turned from her, allowing her to stand. He nudged her away from the other wolves. Arnaaluk departed down the hillside, staring back at him with dread and grief. Her head and tail hung limp and her apprehension mounted at what lay ahead. Thoughts of the dangers that lurked outside their territory tormented her. Thoughts of being mauled to death by a bear or being trampled by a moose, but even worse, she could die a lingering death from starvation in the dead of winter.

Lusa trotted up to her. She kissed her on the muzzle, wishing her good luck in a vain attempt to reassure her.

Arnaaluk loped through the valley, looking back on Payuk and her family. She had longed for this day, and yet now wished it had turned out differently.

Payuk watched as Arnaaluk disappeared into the mountains to the north. His anger turned to an outpouring of love and concern, frustrated by his vain efforts to keep her within the family. His heart longed to run after her, to tell her he was sorry and wished for her to come home, but it was too late. He knew he had to let her go.

For the moment, Payuk was convinced that Arnaaluk could not survive on her own. Despite her rebellion toward him and her lack of maturity, the thought of letting her go made his heart sick. Soon his anxiety turned to guilt and his eyes grew sad as she departed over the horizon.

Lusa sat by his side. "I knew she couldn't stay with us forever," she whispered.

"She is still immature and too sure of herself."

"She's able to survive on her own. I have great faith in her."

"I don't know about that! You have too much faith in her! Most of my pups have left the family. I haven't seen or heard from them since. Who knows what happened to them? Who knows what could happen to her?"

Once Arnaaluk had disappeared from his sight, Payuk grieved. Thoughts overwhelmed him - the image of her being mauled to death by Lycargus, or other dangers she could face.

Kiviaq appeared behind him, whimpering for his sister.

"Don't worry, Kiviaq. She'll be all right."

Kiviaq collapsed to the ground. "Will I ever see her again?"

Payuk sighed. "Probably not. She's chosen to live on her own. Whatever she goes through will be her choice."

Maybe, he thought to himself, *she could survive on her own. Nobody knows.* He was still uncertain. Soon, Payuk pushed his worry about Arnaaluk aside and drifted into a deep sleep, warming his fur with the heat of the afternoon sun.

Chapter Eight

Love at First Sight

Arnaaluk soon overcame her despair and fear of being on her own. She was still worried about the upcoming winter, but she was happy to be free from the rules of her father. Having crossed the rolling hills, she headed back to the mountains in the north, but a good distance from the territory of Lycargus. She took a deep breath and picked up another spruce cone with her teeth.

"I'm glad to be gone," she muttered, trying to convince herself. "He thinks I'm not strong enough to live on my own. He's too worried about me hanging around those 'strange wolves.' Kanak never harmed me once. Neither did that other wolf who risked his life to save me. If I were to ask my father if I could introduce myself to him, would his answer be yes or no? My guess is no. Nevertheless, I won't worry about what he thinks!"

She casually sniffed the forest floor for signs of the other wolf and came across a scent. She assumed the scent was that of the new wolf. She followed it to a clearing in the middle of the forest and there she found him, asleep with a moose antler in his jaws. She approached him carefully, aware that he may not be friendly. She sniffed his fur quietly for confirmation that this was the wolf she sought. Then she stood still, waiting for him to awaken.

At first, he did not rouse, so she gave him a nudge on the back. He awoke with a jolt! Arnaaluk jumped back quickly as he opened his eyes, glanced at her, then gasped.

There she was standing before him, the one he had been dreaming of. Her distinctive looks and scent, her black and shiny fur, and her glowing emerald eyes.

Tulok took a deep breath and stretched his legs. He picked up the antler and dangled it in her face. "Hello there!" he mumbled in a relaxed voice, "You must be from those wolves that live along the great river."

"What wolves?"

"You know who I'm talking about."

"Oh yes! I was from that family. I'm Arnaaluk, what is your name?"

"Tulok! Do you still live with them? Did your father send you away?"

"Well…yes, he did."

"I would like to hear the story of your life. Where were you born? Were you born in that den by the river I passed this morning?"

"No, I was born in the woodlands! My mother couldn't find a den. Why do you ask?"

"Just wondering. I was beginning to suspect that den belonged to your father and mother. Anyway, you're the prettiest little vixen I've ever seen! Your black fur reminds me of the night sky, and your green eyes glisten like the northern lights."

"Well, that's a charming thing to say!" she remarked, "You seem to have an aptitude for flattery."

Arnaaluk grabbed Tulok's antler with her teeth and tried to wrest it away from him, but Tulok held it with his sturdy jaws.

"You're pretty strong!" he said, "Can you take down caribou like I can?"

"Yes, I've taken down a caribou before!"

Tulok tugged at the antler. "Aren't you a little too young to be living on your own? There's a lot to learn about being a wolf. There's a lot to learn about living on your own... like I do."

"You'd better watch me, I'm craftier than any fox. I fight like a bear!"

Arnaaluk felt hesitant to make eye contact with him. She was attracted to the masklike shadows around his eyes and his big, bulky shoulders. There was something about his appearance that appealed to her. He looked like a strong and rugged wolf who could hunt caribou and fight.

Distracted, Arnaaluk lost her grip on the antler.

Tulok pulled it away from her. "No! You can't have it, it's mine!"

He tossed the antler high into the air. Arnaaluk remembered the trickery she learned in her youth. While Tulok held his mouth open, hoping to catch it, she jumped in front of him, snatching it from him.

With the stolen antler in her jaws, Arnaaluk mischievously dashed into the forest.

Tulok rushed after her. "Hey! That's mine!"

Arnaaluk took one last look at him. "I told you… I'm craftier than any fox, eagle eyes! By the way… did you drop something?"

She scurried among the trees, then ran for cover in a thicket. She set the moose antler on the ground and sat beside it. A few raindrops pattered on her head, and she knew that the rain would eventually wash her scent and tracks away.

For the first few moments, Tulok followed her tracks and scent through the trees. Suddenly, there came a rumble of thunder and raindrops fell around him, cleansing the air, ground, and trees. Every scent of moose, grizzly, spruce, and even the scent of Arnaaluk were all washed away. Tulok paused and sniffed the air, but she was nowhere in sight. He crawled into a trench underneath a log, seeking shelter from the sudden downpour.

Soon, the brief cloudburst ended, and a cool mist descended across the forest. Tulok shook all the rainwater from his fur, scanning the trees with his eyes and nose, seeking the young black wolf. She was nowhere in sight.

Tulok came back out into the clearing, resting his body in the wet grass. He thought back upon the times spent with his family, the sounds of their hearty howls and play fights. Homesickness flooded his mind.

As the sky turned to twilight, Tulok glanced over at a mountain to the northeast. He listened for his family's howls, but to no avail. Resting his head on the ground, he watched the crescent moon ascending over the horizon.

Chapter Nine

Lycargus Seeks Revenge

Early in autumn, the weather cooled and a thin layer of snow blanketed the land. Lycargus, roaming the hills along the river, sought his prey. As he ascended the hillside, moose tracks appeared before him and he took a deep breath, inhaling their scent. Lycargus knew herds of moose sought refuge in this area. To his knowledge, Payuk and his family hunted caribou instead of moose, so the moose felt safe here. Knowing the winter was coming, Lycargus knew he and his family needed meat.

A large bull moose trotted in front of him. Lycargus stood still, licking his gums as the hulking creature lumbered through the trees. The moose paused and turned his head to find a single wolf watching him. He picked up speed and cantered up the hillside until he reached the summit. Lycargus knew he could not take down such a large moose on his own, so he rushed back toward the mountains where his family waited for him.

Lycargus' family was gathered on the tall mountain overlooking the river. First to greet him was Alasie, his mate. She was always faithful to him and bore him many offspring. Whenever one of his pups died of starvation or was snatched by an eagle, he mourned with her. She was not only a faithful mate, but also a caring and devoted mother.

Second to greet him was Amak, his youngest brother, the runt of the litter. Amak was always timid and oafish. He was also short and had unusually large paws. Amak approached his brother with his tail tucked, hunched over with respect, licking Lycargus on the muzzle.

Lycargus jumped upon a tall rock, gazing down upon the river's south side. He observed several moose grazing along the river's edge.

Lycargus turned to Amak. "See those moose down there?"

Amak licked his lips. "Yes, I see them, but isn't that the home of Payuk?"

"It is. Moose everywhere, and we will claim the land where they roam! Do you remember a wolf named Alootook? A long time ago, when I was a pup, he blocked access to our hunting grounds. A time of starvation passed, and he and his brothers killed our father and uncle and drove us from our land. We spent an entire winter starving while the moose sought refuge on the great river's south side. When his eldest son, Payuk grew up, he left home and his brother and sister joined him. For seasons, they've lived along the river's edge, marking their territory and declaring to us we shall not pass."

Amak sat on the large boulder next to his older brother. "So...what do we do? Are we taking this land back?"

Lycargus was certain. "We will. First, we must drive Payuk's family out. We must take their land by force and kill all who stand in our way. We are superior in size and strength and those wolves cower at the sight of a moose. Speaking of moose, I've even killed a moose on my own. Of course, it was just a young cow."

"I chewed the flank off a moose once," Amak recalled, "The moose ran away on three legs and I never saw it again."

"And maybe you could do the same to Payuk," joked Lycargus. He snapped the bone in half to symbolize his malicious plan. "But we will warn them first!"

Amak brushed his nose across the ground, picking up the cone of a spruce with his teeth. "We could just move farther to the north…" he suggested.

"Move to the north? Never! If we move too far north, we'll end up in an area full of strong teeth that grab from the ground and catch you by the paw. There are strings that snatch you by the neck and strangle you. I've already lost a son and daughter to such traps. It's also an area teeming with tall figures carrying sticks that bring death - killers!"

Amak brought up another problem. "What about that wolf who's been loitering around our territory?"

Lycargus understood who he meant. "You mean Tulok? The one who's been trying to steal away my daughters?"

"Yes, him!"

"Well, if he persists, we will kill him!"

"He's faster than you are. I was watching you chase him down a steep mountainside, and you slipped and fell."

"Well, who cares about him, anyway? He is the least of my worries."

Lycargus descended the tall rock while Amak howled for the other wolves to summon them. Lycargus joined in as Amak howled, then the other wolves began to howl, as well. Lycargus lowered his nose toward the ground following the moose tracks and climbed a tall rocky ledge overlooking the banks of the river. His howl then changed - a warning directed at Payuk.

Chapter Ten

The First Warning

With the first howls of Lycargus and his family, Payuk and his family paused to listen. For them, it meant only one thing: invaders. Payuk dashed into a nearby forest where he stood listening. Nearby over a dozen wolves howled, which meant this rival group was at least twice the size of his, possibly larger.

Payuk's brother, Akiak, approached him. "What's going on?" he asked.

Payuk shuddered. "It's Lycargus and his family. They're here again."

Akiak turned his ears forward, listening to the howls. "I knew there were many of them. They have a large territory, much larger than ours."

Payuk agreed, "Yes, more wolves mean more living space! Their territory might be three times the size of ours!"

Payuk raised his head and howled at the enemy, warning them to back away. Akiak, Kiviaq, Nova and Lusa also joined in a simultaneous chorus. The cliff walls, the valleys and hills amplified and echoed their voices. The tone of their howls changed with each voice. With rapid modulation, the howl of one wolf became two, and two became four. Four became eight, then five became ten. The echoes multiplied the howls until it was deafening.

Lycargus stood at the edge of the nearby hill. At first, the other wolves in his family backed away. It sounded like a chorus of thirty, fifty, or even a hundred wolves howling before them.

Amak cowered behind Lycargus. "There are too many! More than I thought! There must be a hundred of them!"

Lycargus was not fooled. Unlike his family, he did not shrink back in terror. "No, don't be afraid. There are only six of them. Don't let their howls fool you. I've been watching them from a distance."

Lycargus raised his head and howled in return. The other wolves in his large family howled with him. Their howls likewise multiplied and soon, it was almost as if a thousand wolves were howling at once. The sounds echoed from the hills and the bank of the river.

Once he finished howling, Lycargus listened for a response from the other wolves. Not a sound.

"See? Those wolves didn't respond to our howls. Their attempts to drive us away from these moose-rich lands are futile. This proves we are superior to them," he bragged.

"I notice I didn't hear the voice of that young black wolf mingled among them. What's her name?" asked Amak.

"Arnaaluk! She must've run away. Well, not to worry, eventually I'll run into her. Maybe next time she won't be so lucky."

Payuk shuddered in fear. Lusa tried to reassure him. "Don't be afraid, Payuk. There aren't that many of them."

Payuk was perplexed. "Not just a dozen! More than I thought, maybe thirty or forty!"

Kiviaq cowered before them. "Probably more! Like at least a hundred!"

Payuk turned quickly. "No! Not that many, but more of them than of us! We've got to get out of here!"

Akiak stood vigilant. "No! No, we must stand our ground!"

Lusa, not noted for being a fighter, emphasized their safety. "I don't care how many there are. I don't feel safe here."

She nudged Kiviaq and Nova into the nearby forest. As they fled to safety, Payuk and Akiak stood their ground. They continued to howl back at the invaders, but Payuk didn't know how long he could hold them off.

Chapter Eleven

Another Brush with Death

As the ominous howls of Lycargus sounded across the land, Tulok chased a small herd of caribou. He found them difficult to catch on his own as they were all healthy adults, and the caribou escaped up a nearby hill. Tulok, panting and exhausted, gave up on his swift targets and turned around, trotting away as they vanished over the horizon.

Desperate for food, Tulok plowed his nose through the shallow snow and began to zigzag through the forest. Then, he slowed his pace as he saw Arnaaluk among the trees, curled up in the snow, her tail covering her nose as a veil.

Arnaaluk's eyes slowly blinked open as Tulok serenaded her with a howl. She unraveled and rose to her feet. "Welcome back, Tulok. Still looking for that lost antler? I know where it is."

"No, I don't need it anymore."

Arnaaluk curled her lips and growled at him as if preparing for a playful fight. "I was hoping you were, you must fight me if you want it."

Tulok was impressed by her aggressive look. "A little snappy, aren't you? That's what I like in a female!"

Tulok turned around to find his brother Kanak standing behind him. Kanak stared into his eyes. "What do you want?" Tulok asked.

Kanak circled Arnaaluk. "Stay away from her, she's mine!"

Tulok nipped him on the shoulder as a warning. Kanak yelped and jumped back. It was a strong nip that in times past had kept him at bay.

Arnaaluk gasped. "Kanak! What are you talking about? I don't belong to you!"

Tulok snarled at him, raising the fur on his back. "You heard what she said, Kanak. She doesn't belong to you!"

"She will learn to respect me instead of you, Tulok," said Kanak, "You are a brute!"

"I'm not a brute!" Tulok protested, "Now back down!"

As they snarled at each other, Arnaaluk saw several wolves moving among the trees, tracking prey. She sniffed the air, detecting the scent of Lycargus and his dreaded wolves. The three wolves were surrounded. She nudged Kanak on the back.

"What is it?" he asked.

"Lycargus! I've caught his scent. He's here!"

"Lycargus?" asked Kanak, "What's he doing here? This isn't his territory."

"I guess it's his territory now," added Tulok, "I heard his howls this morning. He's come to reclaim this land. We've got to get out of here or he will kill us. We must split up!"

Arnaaluk agreed. She sniffed the air one more time and looked to the northeast. There he was. She dashed down the hillside, trying to find a place to hide, but there was no rock or tree large enough to conceal her. Arnaaluk sniffed the ground for marked territory, hoping she could cross a border into a safe zone, but she found none. She tried fleeing to the east and then the west, but there were enemy wolves surrounding her. In desperation, she finally found a place to hide, an abandoned bear den. She rushed inside, safe for the moment, but there were two things that could give her away. Her tracks and scent! She hoped Lycargus would never find them.

Lycargus sniffed the air and examined the ground for signs of moose, but the scent of other wolves crossed his nose. He followed the scent to where Arnaaluk, Kanak and Tulok had been. They were all gone, but their tracks still littered the snow. Lycargus sniffed the area, finding the scents of Kanak, Tulok and the scent of…Arnaaluk! The scent was fresh. It was a sign these wolves had been here just a few moments ago. Lycargus followed her tracks until they formed a trail leading downhill. He was on to something.

A breeze picked up, blowing the fresh tracks and scent away from the crusty snow, but Lycargus continued to search. Then, right behind him, there it was. An abandoned bear den. Maybe she was hiding here. Lycargus slowed and approached the den quietly. Once he reached the entrance, he peered inside and saw a black lump of fur on the den's floor. The scent of Arnaaluk was strong and there was no doubt in his mind - this was where she was hiding.

Arnaaluk cowered in the den, curled up in a tight ball, fighting the urge to look outside. She squeezed her eyes shut, and sat motionless, barely able to breathe.

Suddenly, panic overtook her as something pulled her from the den by the scruff of her neck! Arnaaluk's eyes jerked open, her heart pounding rapidly. Would this be the end of her? To her horror, she found it was Lycargus who was dragging her from the den! Arnaaluk, shaking with fear, could not tear away from Lycargus. As she was being dragged outside, she heard another sound. She turned and to her relief, there was Kanak!

Kanak nipped Lycargus on the backside. "Let her go!"

Lycargus wheeled around, ripping a piece of Arnaaluk's fur from her body. His teeth had pierced the skin underneath, leaving a deep, bleeding bite wound on the back of her shoulders. Once released from the grip of his jaws, Arnaaluk backed away slowly. Soon, she was a good distance from the unfolding confrontation and ran in a frantic dash. Once she was far away, she stopped to catch her breath. She looked furtively in every direction for the enemy wolves, but there were none in sight. Panting with relief, she trotted out of the forest and into the open valley before her.

Lycargus spit the piece of black fur into the snow. He snarled and stared Kanak in the face, raising the fur on his back in preparation for a fight.

"You want to pick a fight with me? Don't know whose territory you are intruding into?"

Kanak crouched and bared his teeth. "I didn't know this was your territory, I just so happened to..."

"Stumble across it?" Lycargus interrupted.

"You, you...took the words right out of my mouth. As I was saying, I didn't know this was your territory. I mean...I didn't know you and your family were...claiming this as your land," he jittered.

"Very well," growled Lycargus, "You know what happens to unfortunate fools like you who cross me?"

"You kill them?"

Lycargus curled his lips, baring his strong teeth. "Yes, you're right! Violating my territory is a death sentence! Didn't your father teach you to steer clear of the territory of strange wolves?"

Kanak tried to plead with him. "Please! Spare me! I meant no harm to you or your family. I was just tracking caribou!"

"It doesn't matter!"

"Please! Leave me alone! Don't you have anything better to do?"

"Yes, I have something better to do, but I must deal with you first. After I've dealt with you, I will take out that troublesome father of yours, Payuk."

"Payuk is not my father, you idiot!"

Lycargus snorted and growled even louder. "What did you just call me?"

"Nothing!"

"You're a liar! You called me an idiot! What a very bold thing to say to your enemy when your life is in danger!"

Tulok stood at a distance. Studying Kanak and Lycargus challenging each other, he had been ready to confront Lycargus as he was pulling Arnaaluk from the abandoned den. Now he watched as they crouched and snarled, preparing to fight. He crept behind Lycargus unnoticed, overhearing their conversation.

Lycargus gave one last word to Kanak. "As I said, you've made a fatal mistake!" He placed his teeth by Kanak's neck. "Any last words?"

Kanak stood speechless for a moment. "Kill me if you must, but Arnaaluk just got away from you again."

"Oh, too bad! Do I really care?"

Tulok was puzzled to find his brother confronting Lycargus. Previously, Kanak had run away when faced with such an enemy, but now, that didn't matter - now was the time to distract Lycargus. Tulok suddenly opened his powerful jaws and snapped onto Lycargus' tail. It was a sharp and painful bite, puncturing the skin, but not breaking the bone.

Startled by the sharp pain, Lycargus whipped around. Tulok stood panting behind him.

"You again!" growled Lycargus.

Tulok winked his eye at Kanak, then turned and fled with Lycargus chasing him down the hillside. Turning to the west, he slowed his pace, sensing a strong wind approaching.

"Yes, a strong wind coming from... over there!" he whispered to himself.

A thick cloud of loose, blowing snow rushed toward him.

Tulok picked up his pace. "And here... it... comes!"

A wind of blinding snow engulfed him for a short time, then died down. Tulok paused to catch his breath in the midst of the dense whiteout. When the snow had cleared, he looked behind him. Lycargus was gone.

"He lost me! The slowpoke! Sorry, Lycargus, I'm just too fast for you," he bragged.

Tulok pointed his eyes and nose to the ground, searching for Kanak and Arnaaluk, hoping they were out of danger and accounted for. After searching for some time, he spotted their tracks which led to an open valley where he found them.

Having been lost in a mist of loose blowing snow, Lycargus paused and searched for Tulok. No tracks nor scent. Tulok had disappeared, and Kanak and Arnaaluk were gone, too. It was almost as if his mind had been playing tricks on him. Lycargus growled in frustration as he turned and trotted up the hillside. His ears pricked at the howl of one of his brothers, summoning the wolves to a moose on the other side of the hill.

"If Tulok keeps crossing paths with me, he will regret it!" Lycargus growled to himself.

Amak found him standing by the abandoned bear den. "Lycargus, what are you doing?" he whispered, "We found some moose!"

Forgetting about the three wolves, Lycargus followed his brother and raced to catch up with the others. As he ran, he thought about the hard times he had experienced the past two winters keeping his family alive. For him, many wolves meant many mouths to feed. He thought of the death of his previous mate from starvation, and the time when his eldest brother was found dead and torn to shreds. Payuk or Akiak could have done it. Lycargus and his family never tolerated any rivals.

Hatred welled up in his heart. Those painful and tragic memories fueled his hatred of Payuk. He thought also of Tulok, the pesky young wolf who distracted him once at a crucial time when he was hunting moose – a time when his family relied on him the most. He remembered the tragedies his family experienced - the brutal killing of his father, and the subsequent death of his mother from starvation. Hunting moose meant he did not have to watch his family suffer from hunger. The hunt quickly became his only focus, as he raced downhill.

Chapter Twelve

Skill and Strategy

Having escaped the clutches of Lycargus, Arnaaluk scanned for signs of caribou. She searched for the Porcupine herd, the fabled herd that roamed through these parts during the days of autumn. Suddenly, a large shadow loomed before her. She recognized its shape - the shape of a bull moose, the largest and most dangerous animal she knew of. She crouched then froze, fearful of such a large, hulking creature.

As she tried to back away, the moose turned its head toward her. Snorting, the moose scraped the snow with its front hoof, preparing to charge. It raised its nose in the air and chased Arnaaluk through the forest.

With her tail between her legs, Arnaaluk bolted through the dense trees to slow the large creature in pursuit. Its bulky body and antlers could not pass through the heavy concentration of spruce, and Arnaaluk turned around to find that the moose had lost her. These trees were her saving grace.

She dashed through the thick forest until she reached a safe distance. *Those legs were powerful*, she thought to herself. *Those hooves were big and sharp.* She trembled at the horror of being trampled to death or kicked by a moose.

Arnaaluk reached the edge of the forest and stood on a cliff overlooking a nearby valley, where Tulok and Kanak were waiting for her.

Tulok saw her panting with exhaustion. "What happened to you?"

"I was looking for caribou, but I almost got myself killed!" she panted.

"Did a moose chase you?"

"A moose, indeed."

Tulok understood her fear from his own experiences with moose. "You'd better watch out for them. You get into their territory, and they chase you down and trample you. They'll break every bone in your body."

"I've had two brushes with death today!" she exclaimed. "I'd like to rest a while."

"Don't rest too long. I've just found caribou scent, some tracks, too. If my instincts are correct, we must travel farther north because there are many moose in this area."

"Yes, I know," she added, "These moose have been driven south to the river by Lycargus and his family. The moose are trying to get away from them."

Tulok agreed. "That's just what caribou do when we expand our territory. They flee from us."

While Arnaaluk was resting, Tulok scanned the herd of caribou. He spent the afternoon observing them from a lofty boulder overlooking the snowy hills. As time passed, caribou were filling the valley below.

When evening came, Tulok stood and stretched his legs, then descended the mountainside, creeping toward the herd. He and Arnaaluk both spotted a calf standing alongside its mother. He looked far ahead of the herd, setting his sights upon a dry streambed, full of rocky ground. Tulok had a strategy. "Go after that single calf, Arnaaluk!" he ordered. "Let's drive them toward the streambed."

When the chase began, Tulok and Kanak rushed into the midst of the stampede. With the caribou on either side trying to avoid them, Tulok split the back of the herd in two. To his right, he drove several caribou toward the rocky ground. They stumbled over the rocks.

As the calf fell over on its side, Tulok watched Arnaaluk seize it by the flank. He rushed toward the calf and circled it. The calf kicked Arnaaluk in the mouth, causing her to lose her grip, but Tulok stayed on its trail. It turned the other way, trying to flee from him, but stumbled again over a nearby rock. The calf now stood before him, shivering in fear and breathing heavily. Its mother tried to intervene on its behalf, but the three wolves were in her way.

Tulok crouched low, locking his gaze upon the calf, then jumped forward. He opened his mouth and snatched the calf by the neck, latching onto the throat with his teeth. Streams of blood poured from the open wounds in the calf's neck, dripping in the snow.

The calf's mother stood frozen with shock. As she retreated from the valley with the rest of the herd, Tulok watched her warily. He held the calf's throat in his jaws, listening to its last bleats of agony. Its voice faded to silence as it breathed its last, ending its short life. Tulok released its neck and panted, licking the blood from his teeth.

"How did you learn to do that?" asked Arnaaluk.

"Do what?"

"Herd those caribou onto rocky ground."

Tulok explained. "It's simple! It's a tactic I learned from my father. It's just those simple hunting strategies we learn from our elders over time. Caribou differ from us. They follow the majority of the herd, moving around as a group with no central direction. They're not a complex family unit like we are. We think as individuals. We cooperate with each other as a family. That's how hunting works in our culture. Understood? No one can herd a family of wolves!"

Arnaaluk grabbed the calf by the flank. "Yes, I know that. I learned that from the time I was young."

Tulok placed his paws on the carcass. "Sometimes we all need someone to refresh our memory."

As Tulok prepared to take the first bite, Kanak jumped on top of him, giving him a powerful bite to the shoulder. Tulok snapped at him and snarled, and Kanak backed away. He dropped his head and lowered his tail in a crouched position before his older brother.

"Stay away from the calf, it's mine!" Tulok growled.

Kanak backed away from him. He whimpered at Tulok, pleading with him to allow him to eat, but Tulok stood with his shoulders hunched, his lips curled, and the fur on his back raised. Kanak backed farther away until Tulok's face returned to normal. With the other two wolves enjoying their meal, he waited, listening to each crack and crunch. He sulked in the snow, with no share in the kill Tulok had made. He waited until they were finished eating.

Chapter Thirteen

Hungry and Lonely

Once the other two wolves finished eating, Kanak took one last look at the carcass. Nothing left but hair and hooves. A dozen ravens were picking off the last pieces of meat. Kanak was desperate. He licked the blood from the snow, but none of it could satisfy his hunger. With his head slumped and his legs weak, he retreated from the scene of the kill, still anxious for food.

Kanak followed the tracks of the other two wolves to their resting site. He approached Arnaaluk as she lay next to Tulok.

Tulok snarled at him. "Leave her alone!"

Kanak backed away from Tulok. He kept himself as far from them as possible, resting his sore legs and paws in the snow. Kanak's belly was empty and he struggled to close his eyes and let his mind rest. He laid awake, staring at Arnaaluk. Every moment he spent watching her made his heart sick. He turned his head away, trying to ignore her as much as possible.

Kanak gazed at the twilight sky, watching the Canada geese migrating south. The geese were joined by small flocks of tundra swans. He noted their strange formations, the shape of a V and the shape of an X, sometimes the shape of a Y. On the south slope of a nearby mountain, a bear entered its den in preparation for its winter slumber. The dark blue sky turned black, then a bright flash of green light shone before him. The beauty of the Aurora Borealis danced across the night sky. The lights flashed their bright colors of green, blue, and yellow. Soon, the ambience of the moment was shattered by the menacing howls of Lycargus and his family, the sounds resonated from the hills along the river.

Kanak listened carefully to their howls, recognizing the voice of Lycargus mingled among them. He sighed with exasperation, curled his lips and growled. He was aware that these wolves were enemies of the one he loved, remembering how Lycargus tried to kill Arnaaluk the day he met her.

The howls of the enemy wolves aroused Arnaaluk from her sleep. She glanced at the forests along the river. Worried about her two brothers, Kiviaq and Nova, she whimpered, tempted to howl a warning to them, but she hesitated for fear it would give her location away to Lycargus. The howls, much closer to the river than she thought, translated to a threat against her loved ones. It was clear Lycargus was closing in on her family. She could not rejoin them, and she was safer outside the territory of Lycargus. There was no reason for her to travel to the river and put her own life at risk. Maybe being released from home was for her own good.

Once again, the howl of Payuk reached Arnaaluk's ears. It was a warning for her not to come this way. A warning not to come back home. The howl told her that Lycargus' family was large, strong, and robust. She would not stand a chance against them. The best strategy was to stay where she was. Arnaaluk clung to the frail hope the day would never dawn when she heard the dreaded sound of mournful howls from her family. Or maybe their howls would cease forever. Horrific images flashed through her mind - the bodies of her father, uncle, aunt, and brothers mutilated and ripped to shreds.

She turned to look at Tulok. "I want you to know how very grateful I am that Kanak saved my life," she said. "He came running to me when Lycargus was about to kill me. Maybe he is brave after all."

"He cannot fight Lycargus," Tulok replied. "Lycargus is too strong for him. The only reason he escaped was because I nipped him on the tail."

"Nevertheless, I am not fully impressed with you, Tulok. You don't seem to have kindness toward him. Why did you make him to go hungry?"

"I want him to leave us! I don't want him here!"

"I don't care! He's your brother and you will treat him with respect," she growled.

"We fought constantly as pups!" said Tulok.

With no more words to speak, Arnaaluk got up and moved away.

Trying to take her mind off Lycargus, she contemplated what could be done to improve her hunting skills. She knew it hadn't been wise to break with the family before her hunting skills had fully matured. She longed to return to them, but it was impossible. Listening to the howls along the river, she knew her family was surrounded. They were in danger and she could not go back.

The next day, on a chilly autumn morning, a small flock of ravens gathered overhead. Arnaaluk followed them to a small stream. The ravens converged on the carcass of a caribou. The caribou appeared healthy, the only bites and blemishes were made by the ravens' beaks. It was most likely dead from natural causes, and Arnaaluk grabbed the carcass by the side, dragging it out of the water.

A young grizzly bear had also laid claim to the caribou. It was not a full-grown adult, still an adolescent, so not as deadly or vicious. The bear approached the carcass and tugged on its hide. Arnaaluk snarled at the bear, then nipped it on its front paw. The bear did not let the carcass go, so Arnaaluk nipped the bear again, this time on the front legs and shoulders. She dashed to the rear end of the bear and gave it another nip to the rump. The irritated grizzly took swipes at Arnaaluk with his powerful paws, but Arnaaluk was swift, dodging each attack. Arnaaluk continued to circle the bear, biting his legs and thighs, and after enduring multiple bites, the bear retreated.

Once the bear was gone, Arnaaluk panted with a smug expression on her face. Having fended off a bear on her own, Arnaaluk dragged the carcass out of the stream. She howled, calling the other two wolves to the scene. While she was waiting for them, a sense of pride overcame her. She thought to herself that maybe she *could* fend off an adult grizzly on her own, even though it was not logically possible for her, and also very dangerous. She decided this was no time to fight with bears. Now was the time to eat.

Kanak dashed toward the carcass. He was desperate for food. He had nothing to eat for the past three days, not even the calf

Tulok had caught yesterday. He found Tulok already feasting on the carcass. Desperate for food, Kanak approached him.

Tulok snapped at him. "Stay away from the carcass!"

Arnaaluk scolded him. "Do you want to starve your own brother to death?"

Tulok nudged him to the caribou's left shoulder. Overwhelmed with starvation, Kanak ripped out a chunk of flesh, gnawing on the shank, devouring the meat.

"Now you've eaten your share!" Tulok growled, "Get lost!"

Kanak backed away from the carcass. He watched as Tulok devoured the loins and flank, filling his belly with more than he could eat.

The memory played back in his mind once again - his upbringing with his family. Just before he left home, Kanak had tried to catch caribou on his own, but failed and bore the guilt of losing three of his siblings to starvation. In time, he grew to maturity, but was meek and scarred. He wandered among the rolling hills by the Yukon River, eating anything he could find. He would often starve for days, chasing caribou to no avail. For a time, he sought solace along the banks of the river. To him, it was a peaceful area, far away from the windy valleys and avalanches that plagued the mountains to the north. It was the howls of Arnaaluk and her family, and the lure of abundant caribou that drew him here.

Kanak placed his paw over his muzzle. He closed his eyes as Tulok consumed the back legs and the other flank, stuffing himself until half the carcass was consumed. While Tulok relaxed and closed his eyes, drifting off into a nap, Kanak stayed alert.

Creeping over to the carcass, he quietly chewed until his energy was restored.

That evening, as the three wolves guarded what was left of the carcass, Arnaaluk was still hungry. As she went back for more, ravens swarmed the carcass - so dense she could not penetrate the flock without being pestered or pecked. A bald eagle joined them, picking at the flesh with his sharp beak. When she came near, the eagle made sharp chirping sounds, intimidating her away from its food.

Arnaaluk decided she had eaten enough. She retreated, leaving the carcass to the scavengers. Kanak, seeing that Tulok was asleep, sat next to her. Being mistrustful of him, she backed away. She was eager to avoid him at every opportunity.

"Please stay away from me!" she whimpered.

"Why? Do you not like me?"

"No, it's just… I…" she hesitated to answer.

She moved her resting spot a good distance from him.

After a brief nap, Kanak yawned and trotted away from the other two wolves. Standing in the open valley, he kept his eyes on the stars in the sky. Still wide awake, he leapt and rolled in the snow. He grabbed a tree branch, tossing it a great distance. He rolled and tossed a spruce cone as if it were a vole. A time of play temporarily took his mind off the loneliness that plagued him.

He glanced at the two wolves and the carcass they were guarding. He collapsed to the ground, moping as he tried to stop thinking about Arnaaluk. He watched as a porcupine hobbled through the valley a few feet away from him, and the peculiar shapes the migratory geese formed in the evening sky, wishing he, too, were high above the ground. He closed his eyes and tried to sleep, but could not.

A great horned owl flew into a tree overlooking him and gazed upon the landscape, shouting his familiar call, Whoo! Whoo! Lying half-awake, Kanak opened one of his eyes, glaring at the owl. After he closed his eyes, the call sounded again, Whoo! Whoo!

Kanak jerked one eye open, growling at the owl. Then, something caught his attention. He heard something moving beneath the snow - a vole? Kanak pawed the snow. He looked up at the owl, watching as it prepared to swoop down and snatch the hapless prey in its talons. The closeness of the vole to his paw's reach gave him an advantage over the owl. He thought of this as an object lesson. To him, that owl was just like Tulok, and the vole as Arnaaluk's affection. He intended to use this to prove he could win Arnaaluk from him. He bent his neck to the snow, opening his mouth, ready to pluck the vole from its cover. Suddenly, the owl swooped down, snatching it from his reach.

It was a foolish object lesson. Kanak sighed, then watched as the owl crushed and kneaded the vole in midair. The owl flew back into the tree, holding the vole in its beak as to taunt the wolf lying below.

The encounter with the owl was enough to dampen his spirits and hurt his pride. Kanak tossed and turned in the snow. He was unable to relax, but eventually, his mind settled and he drifted off to sleep.

Chapter Fourteen

Payuk Meets His Fate

Fast asleep after an evening spent tracking caribou, Payuk trembled and awoke with a gasp. In a dream, he heard Arnaaluk yelping, then silence. Alarmed that Arnaaluk was in pain, he feared something had happened to her and jumped from his spot. Frantically, he dashed over a nearby hill. He howled in the air, calling for her, but there was no answer. He found her tracks in the snow, trailing downhill.

Payuk recognized the tracks of Lycargus, mingled among those of Arnaaluk. When he reached the scene of the bear den, he discovered a ghastly sight. A piece of black fur and a few drops of blood. He looked ahead to see more wolf tracks littering the ground further downhill. Payuk's heart nearly stopped, and he trembled in agony.

"Arnaaluk! What's happened to her?" he cried.

He picked up the piece of fur and took it back to the other wolves. He approached Lusa and Akiak with the fur in his mouth as they stood by the side of the river, waiting for him.

Lusa gasped in shock. "What happened?"

Payuk dropped the piece of fur on the ground. "It's Arnaaluk! Lycargus killed her! All I found of her was a piece of fur and a few drops of blood."

"How do you know this?" Lusa asked, "Did you find her body?"

"No, but I know they've killed her! I found a piece of her fur near an old bear den."

Payuk collapsed in grief. Lusa gave him a few kisses on the head to comfort him.

"Don't be upset," she whispered, "Perhaps she was bitten by him, but escaped."

Payuk was not convinced. Lusa placed her paw on the back of his neck. "Don't despair, Payuk. Akiak and I are here for you."

Payuk struggled in grief all night and could not sleep. He refused to move, breathing heavily and shivering with remorse. He felt as if he had wronged his own daughter by being harsh with her. Now she was gone forever, or so he believed. Akiak and Lusa both huddled with him to soothe the grief that overwhelmed him, but it was no use.

From that time, Payuk's health began to fail. His body weakened as he sat by the river and he would not rise or eat. Every night, he would howl because of the fate of his daughter. Sometimes a hopeful thought crossed his mind that she could possibly still be alive. In this case, he would howl a warning to her not to come back home and stay where she was. Nonetheless, there was little hope left in him. Payuk was a pessimist at heart and did not believe his daughter could have lasted this long in a dangerous world by herself.

One morning, the warmth of the sunrise cast its heat upon Payuk's fur. He stood on a tall boulder at the edge of Lycargus'

territory, keeping the invaders at bay. He tried to frighten them with confrontational howls. Payuk knew he could not hold them off forever. Alert to the ever-looming danger, he watched for any sign of Lycargus. For a time, there was silence, but the wait was not long.

Payuk watched Lusa pacing, looking to the left and right. A breeze blew in his face carrying the scent of the enemy. Payuk motioned to her, and Lusa turned to him, howling at the enemy wolves. Akiak, Payuk, Kiviaq, and Nova joined in.

Lusa stood in front of Kiviaq and Nova, guarding them. "They're here! We must leave this place!"

Payuk considered his options. "You must flee! Don't look back!"

The wolves made one last howl at the invaders in solidarity, then Payuk watched in horror as wolves emerged from among the trees. The number of wolves by Lycargus' side doubled, then tripled. Perplexed, he stared at them. He crouched low with his tail pointed straight back as he prepared to fight them to the death. Fleeing from them would not be an option.

Payuk sighed and lowered his head. He was wracked with guilt over his daughter, his legs ached and his heart was weak. He gazed upon Lycargus and the immense size of his family. He stood in the face of death, preparing to fight them.

"Payuk! Are you coming with us?" whispered Lusa frantically.

Payuk did not answer as he gazed upon the wolves converging upon him. Ever since the death of his mate, Payuk

70

had lost all reason to live, and now his daughter was gone too. It was his fault. It was all over. He decided this was where his life would end. He felt sorry for letting his daughter go. "Arnaaluk. I'm so sorry," he whispered.

Suddenly, he looked behind to find Lusa, Kiviaq, and Nova gone. Lycargus jumped on his back, unleashing a powerful bite to the shoulders. He then stared Payuk in the face. "Your family has fled! You are helpless before me! No one can save you now!"

But Akiak was there and confronted the enemy wolf. "If you want to fight my brother, you must fight me!"

"No problem!" Lycargus replied.

The other wolves leapt on Akiak, fiercely mauling him. Akiak tried to fight back, but it was no use as the enemy wolves overwhelmed him. Akiak wrapped himself around Amak's neck, trying to restrain him, but he was no match. Their ferocity was too much for him, and he collapsed in the snow, severely wounded.

Payuk screamed out to him, "Akiak, what are you doing here? Flee with the others!"

Lycargus gave Payuk a powerful bite to his throat, as two other wolves tore lumps from his fur.

"You will pay the ultimate price for stealing our hunting grounds," Lycargus growled, "You will pay for the deaths of my siblings. This is for the time I spent watching them die from starvation."

Lycargus and the other wolves furiously ripped apart his flesh. The scene degenerated into a frenzy of mauling and yelping.

In his final moments, Payuk turned to look at his brother, mauled and bloodied. He grieved for his daughter and what he believed had become of her. He had refused the option of fleeing this territory. He considered himself a part of this land, and this land to be a part of himself. He whimpered in anguish and pain, as the other wolves ripped him open.

Lusa led Kiviaq and Nova over a nearby hill and through the woodlands. They were far away from the scene of carnage.

Lusa paused, panting. "Wait! Let's stop!"

She waited for a moment, turning her head and listening to the yelps in the distance.

"No! No! He's dead! They killed him!" she cried.

"What's happened?" asked Kiviaq.

Lusa nudged him away. "Please, let's keep moving!"

The three wolves raced frantically through the woods, each moment seemed an eternity. Lusa worried for her brothers. Before long, she and her two nephews reached the valley at the end of the forest. For the moment, they were far away from the clutches of Lycargus. They paused to catch their breath in the open valley and stood in silence. Akiak and Payuk were not coming with them.

By their instincts, they understood Akiak and Payuk's fate. Lusa trembled and collapsed in grief. A few moments of silence passed, then the air calmed and everything stood still. She broke out into a mournful howl for Payuk and Akiak, then Kiviaq and Nova joined in. The three wolves united in a somber chorus of eerie howls that permeated through the air.

Chapter Fifteen

A Time to Mourn

Early that afternoon, Arnaaluk tossed a spruce cone in a nearby forest until eerie sounds caught her attention. The howls of her family, low-pitched and somber. Her heart and stomach fluttered with fear as she realized something terrible had happened. Rushing toward the open valley, she kept her nose open for the family scent. She dashed through the woodlands and up the steep hill, crossing into enemy territory. She caught her breath, as the scent of Lycargus reached her nose.

She sniffed the ground for signs of her father and found his tracks scattered across the light snow. His scent amplified around her when she reached a clearing where flocks of ravens descended from the sky. Rushing toward the source of their attention, she found them swirling around a particular spot.

Shock resonated through her. She stopped in her tracks, fearing the worst as she looked at the ground. The tracks of enemy wolves littered the snow, mingled with those of her father. Before her was the horrific scene of ravens feasting on a carcass that was mutilated beyond recognition, but clearly that of a wolf.

Spatters and puddles of blood littered the snow, mingled with lumps of dark gray fur. Arnaaluk shivered as she surveyed the grisly scene. She hesitated to inhale its scent, fearing it to be one of her family. Maybe her father.

Arnaaluk mustered the courage to sniff the carcass, and the identity was confirmed. It *was* her father, torn to pieces and dead! Shock flowed through her, jolting her heart and pulsing across her body. She sniffed the tracks littered throughout the snow. These were the tracks of Lycargus. She listened as his victory howls filled the air.

Arnaaluk then caught sight of her uncle, Akiak, lying in the snow, badly wounded. His body was covered in bite wounds. She rushed toward him, picking him up by the scruff of his neck with her teeth.

Akiak whimpered to her in a faint voice. "Arnaaluk! You're alive! Your father was sure you were dead!"

"Come with me! I've got to get you out of here before Lycargus returns."

"No, please! Just go! Run for your life! You can't save me!"

These were his last words. Arnaaluk nudged Akiak, goading him to awaken, but it was no use. She turned and ran from the scene of carnage, leaving the bodies of her father and uncle behind. As she rushed downhill and through the valley, she listened to the howls of the enemy. With each howl, she picked up her pace. Her body shook with grief and dread.

At last, she arrived back in the valley. She breathed a sigh of relief, safe from danger. After catching her breath, she heard Lusa howling. Relieved to hear she was alive, she followed the howl to a valley on the eastern side.

There she found Lusa with her two brothers. They were gathered out in the open, grieving. Nova was pacing aimlessly.

Lusa had climbed to a tall, rocky ledge overlooking the valley, howling in mourning for her brothers. Kiviaq lay on the ground in a daze. Their time stood still.

Arnaaluk wandered among the mourning wolves. None of them greeted her or even paid attention to her presence. They sat speechless, paralyzed with grief and shock. She looked upon her brother, Kiviaq, as he sat motionless in the wet grass. Glancing at his sad face, she whimpered with compassion and settled next to him. From time to time, she tried to lick him on the head to comfort him, but it was no use.

Arnaaluk had little respect for her father when he was alive, but now she harbored a sense of solidarity with the family in their sorrow. She pressed against her brother, and nuzzled the side of Kiviaq's head with affection.

Over the days that followed, she risked her life ascending the nearby hill along the river to see the area where her father and uncle were killed. There she would lay, grieving for them. From time to time, the wind blew and the snow fell, covering their carcasses. Each time, she knew she could not stay here long. She knew that at any moment, Lycargus could come out of the nearby forest.

During the night, the sky filled with clouds and a cold light rain drizzled over the land. As tiny drops of water tingled on her, Arnaaluk shivered in the cold. The patches of snow surrounding her gradually turned to ice, and the soil turned to frozen mud. The weather fit the mood of another long and dreary evening.

For the first time in Arnaaluk's life, she was overcome with love for her father. She thought back with regret to the time she broke with the family, when her father reproved her for wandering away. Now she whimpered and howled for him, her anger now a distant memory. Arnaaluk had not felt such sadness since the day her mother had died, and a renewed feeling of grief and sympathy swept over her. She was beginning to understand the love and loyalty necessary within a wolf family.

The light rain grew colder and the temperature dropped below freezing. The rain turned to sleet, and then to snow. The wolves remained deep in the valley, howling in mourning and wandering aimlessly for days. Their bodies grew gaunt with hunger.

One morning, Arnaaluk and the other wolves left the valley and wandered to the northeast across the rolling hills. They trekked to the mountains, where the high icy snow-covered peaks stood before them. Wisps of loose snow blew across their summits and gusts of wind swept across the valleys, creating an eerie howling sound. In the evening, the wolves paused to rest after a long day's journey.

Chapter Sixteen

Welcome to the Family

Still distraught from the death of her father, Arnaaluk was in no mood to hunt or play. Kiviaq licked her on the cheek, but this did not comfort her. She felt guilty for leaving her father, and languished in depression. Kiviaq left for a time to hunt for food and brought her a snowshoe hare, laying it by her front paws. Having no appetite, Arnaaluk ignored it and left it laying in the snow.

Kiviaq searched the valley for anything that could satisfy his hunger. To his relief, he found the front shoulders, neck and head of a caribou lying beside a frozen stream. Kiviaq was desperate for food, and didn't care if other wolves had claimed it. With no hesitation, he began ripping off fur and nibbling on the hide. Suddenly, Kiviaq found another wolf standing over the carcass. He jumped with shock and his heart fluttered.

"Who are you? And what are you doing here?" the strange wolf asked.

"Please! I don't mean you any harm!"

"I know you don't. I am Kanak! What is your name?"

"Kiviaq."

Kiviaq crouched before the strange wolf as he sniffed his fur. There was no other wolf in sight, so obviously this was a lone wolf.

"Stop! Do him no harm! He's my brother!"

Kanak turned to find Arnaaluk standing behind him. He breathed a sigh of relief.

"Arnaaluk! Where have you been?" asked Kanak, "I've been looking for you!"

"I've been back with my family. Lycargus killed my father."

Kiviaq backed away from Kanak, maintaining his distance. Kanak stood in front of Arnaaluk but continued to glare at Kiviaq. By instinct, he knew what this behavior signified.

"You already have a mate?" Kiviaq asked Arnaaluk.

"No," she replied. "I don't belong to him."

The mournful howls of Lusa and Nova interrupted their conversation. Kiviaq howled back, letting them know he was there, then turned and trotted back to the other wolves.

Arnaaluk tried to follow Kiviaq, but Kanak snatched her by the scruff of the neck. "Where do you think you're going?"

"I need to get back to my family."

"No! You will stay with me!"

"I can't stay with you," she protested. "My family needs me! They can't hunt caribou as well as I can! They need my help or they will starve."

Arnaaluk did not trust either Tulok or Kanak - Kanak was a coward and Tulok was an oppressor. For now, she decided she would be better off either independent or with those she loved.

She trotted through the valley to find the other wolves, but Kanak followed her.

"Don't you have anything better to do?" she asked.

"Please, don't leave me!" pleaded Kanak.

"Why?"

"I need you!"

"You'll have to do better than that."

Arnaaluk ignored him. She approached the other wolves and returned to the site where they camped. With Kanak following her, she climbed to the top of a tall rock in the middle of the valley.

Arnaaluk snarled at him, demanding that he leave. "Please go! This is not your family!"

Kanak refused. "I won't leave you! Please let me stay!"

"Okay! You can stay with us. You are free to be part of my family. Just leave me alone!"

"You mean to tell me you don't like me?"

For a moment, Arnaaluk hesitated to answer. "I just want to be left alone! Is that clear? My father is dead and my family needs me."

Kanak did not leave. He wandered among the other wolves, sniffing them. He first sniffed Lusa, the creamy white wolf seated next to the tall rock. He turned to Nova and did the same. Kanak circled around Arnaaluk, and stood over her, staring and curling his lips at the others.

"Soon, you will learn to accept me as your mate," he whispered to her.

"Why should I?" she snapped, "You're a poor hunter. If you take me as your mate, you'll depend on me for your survival. Is this what you want?"

"Yes!" he growled.

"How did you survive on your own for such a long time?" she asked.

"I fed off dead caribou. I may not be good at chasing and killing a caribou, but I'm a good scavenger. I can certainly find a good carcass."

"Well, that's not good enough," Arnaaluk uttered. She closed her eyes and rested her head.

Having heard mournful howls for the past few days, Tulok became curious. He found Arnaaluk and Kanak resting together on a tall rock, overlooking the other three wolves. At first, he kept his distance. Strangely, he noticed none of them charged him as an intruder. They were too shocked and grieved to defend their own territory. After mustering up the courage to approach them, he nuzzled Arnaaluk on the shoulder, but she did not respond. He wandered among the mourning wolves, and like his brother, sniffed each of them, storing their distinct scents in his memory.

Later that day, Tulok laid on the ground, hungry from a lack of caribou. He was jolted by a nip to the tail.

Nova was standing behind him. Tulok nudged him away. "Leave me alone, please!"

Nova nuzzled Tulok on the shoulder and back. Tulok sighed and growled. Irritable, he nipped the young wolf on the shoulder.

Nova yelped and backed away from him. "I'm sorry! I didn't mean to bother you."

Tulok paid no attention to him and sat resting in the frosty grass. Still trying to win his attention, Nova gave him one lick to the muzzle.

"What are you doing here? Where are you from?" he asked.

At first, Tulok was hesitant to answer him. "My name is Tulok," he said, "I come from around these parts. Arnaaluk, and my brother, Kanak, brought me here. Arnaaluk especially. I don't care much for Kanak."

"I am Nova, Arnaaluk is my sister. So, what about that brother of yours?"

"Let's just say I don't particularly like him."

At first, Tulok felt uncomfortable next to a stranger, but by instinct, he knew he wanted to belong to something greater than himself - a family. Although he rested among the mourning wolves, Tulok could not sleep. He swayed his head back and forth, sniffing for caribou. He kept his eyes alert, watching the nearby forest.

Chapter Seventeen

The Value of Teamwork

Another long polar night descended across the land. Arnaaluk left the other wolves to hunt caribou. Still weak with grief, she stood on a tall mountain and gazed into the vast valley before her. Setting her sights on a caribou separated from the herd, she descended the mountain, stalking and then chasing it. Suddenly, the caribou turned and charged her, its front hooves trampling her. She yelped, then turned and ran.

Still lacking the adequate skills to catch a caribou on her own, Arnaaluk retreated to the nearby forest. She slinked through the woods and into a clearing, then sniffed for voles. She used her front paws to pat the snow cover. Detecting movement underneath, she made a vertical leap high in the air, but missed her target on the first try.

She inched her paws forward and again detected the same vole. With a second vertical leap she landed with her front paws, crushing and paralyzing the vole on impact. She pushed her nose into the snow, drawing out a single vole. She tossed it in the air and caught it with her jaws. She chewed on the dead vole, then swallowed it.

Again, Arnaaluk plowed her nose through the snow. She caught a second vole as it was getting away, then detected a third vole. She held the second vole in her mouth while chomping on the snow in pursuit of the third vole. She caught it and swallowed both voles at the same time. Arnaaluk made a third vertical leap, catching another vole. She tossed it in the air and caught it with her teeth.

Not far from her, a fox emerged from its hole and scampered to the vole-rich hunting site. While Arnaaluk was poking her nose into the snow to catch a fifth vole, the pesky vixen dove headfirst into the snow, snatching it from her. Arnaaluk raised her head and glared at the fox. She took a few steps to the left and pawed the snow cover, feeling another vole moving underneath. Again, the fox pounced in front of her, snatching it. The fox scurried across the snow, taking one vole after another.

Arnaaluk nipped at the fox, trying to make it drop the last vole. The fox, being slender, agile, and somewhat mischievous, ran underneath her. Arnaaluk lost her balance and toppled, landing in the snow with a thud. As she got back on her feet, the fox stared at her with amusement. While Arnaaluk was still hungry, the greedy fox rushed back into her hole, satisfied and well-fed.

Frustrated, Arnaaluk sniffed the snow for more voles, desperately plowing up every inch. Soon, everything hidden beneath the snow became visible, but no more luck. She plowed her muzzle through the snow and ate vast quantities of it, but she was still hungry. Voles were a secondary food source. No wolf could survive on voles alone, she knew she must catch large game.

Arnaaluk was weary with grief and hunger. Moaning in pain, her legs ached and she collapsed in the snow. She listened for the sound of caribou, but for now, none could be seen or heard. She closed her eyes and tried to sleep, but her empty stomach kept her awake.

For now, all hope seemed lost. In desperation, Arnaaluk sniffed the air one last time. She smelled something familiar. Caribou? Is this what she thought it was? She followed the scent to a small clearing in the forest, where she paused to hear the howl of another wolf. By its tone, she knew it was Tulok, and she understood he was trailing this herd. She howled back to let him know she was on her way.

First came the scent, then came the tracks. Watching the tracks and following the scent, Arnaaluk was in hot pursuit. She steered clear of the borders where Lycargus had marked his territory and listened for another howl from Tulok.

The next morning, Arnaaluk reached the banks of the great river. Heavy snow was falling, the temperature was rapidly dropping, and the river frozen to ice. Most of the ice was thick enough to support a large caribou. Arnaaluk listened to the ice creaking under the pressure of caribou hooves. The herd she encountered was part of the great Porcupine herd, vast in number and size.

With the first caribou scent carried on the wind, Tulok became fully alert. He desperately followed the scent and tracks with optimism. Although he possessed the skills necessary for hunting caribou, Tulok understood he still needed help to tackle a large bull. He now needed a caribou large enough to feed not only himself, but also five other wolves. The caribou were coming toward him.

Tulok reached the western edge of the forest by the river. Small numbers of caribou passed in the distance. He scrutinized each of them, licking his gums. He had spent the entire night in pursuit of this herd, tracking them to the shores of the river where they gathered. He watched the trees along the river, waiting for Arnaaluk to emerge. Tulok had killed many caribou on his own, but more than one wolf would be needed to take down prey of this size.

Arnaaluk singled out a bull on the left edge of the herd. Tulok was nowhere in sight, but she had no time to lose. She crept toward the bull, then picked up speed. The bull stepped on a weak spot, and the ice underneath him gave way. Plunging into the water with a splash, the bull tried to swim away, but Arnaaluk dove into the icy river and swam after him. With her powerful teeth she seized the bull in the hindquarters. It was not enough as the caribou was an excellent swimmer. One wolf latching onto his hindquarters could not slow him down.

From the corner of her eye, Arnaaluk saw Tulok darting toward the icy river. She held on as he plunged in and swam to the front of the caribou, latching onto its throat and pulling its head underwater. With the jaws of a wolf clamped onto his throat and water filling his lungs, the caribou struggled for his life. Arnaaluk and Tulok kept him restrained until all struggle had ceased.

The two wolves dragged the caribou's lifeless body back to shore. To make sure it was dead, Arnaaluk nudged it with her nose and jumped back. She nudged a second time staring at the caribou, watching every last reflex on the legs and hooves. Arnaaluk was ready for a mouthful of fresh venison. She shook the icicles off her fur. To express her gratitude, she gave Tulok a lick to the muzzle.

The other wolves who had been following Arnaaluk, Tulok and the herd, emerged from the forest. When the time came to eat, Arnaaluk had no father to keep her in line. With Payuk gone, she was now the first to eat. She snarled at Kiviaq and Nova, warning them to back off, before she granted them permission to feed.

As soon as Arnaaluk and the other wolves finished eating, they rested in the snow along the edge of the forest. Arnaaluk curled up, using her tail to shield her eyes from the loose blowing snow. She was fatigued from her hard work hunting caribou.

Chapter Eighteen

The Wolf Song

Arnaaluk slipped into a deep sleep on a full stomach, the most peaceful sleep she'd had in a long time. Having recovered from the grief of her father's death, her life was almost back to normal. That evening, she awoke, partially buried in the shifting snow. Stretching her legs and shaking the snow from her body, she was full of energy. Ascending to the summit of a nearby mountain, she watched a scenic panorama of the Yukon River. She spent the evening gazing upon the majesty of the moon, stars and the Aurora Borealis.

Arnaaluk listened as other wolves howled from far away. Some wolves were preparing for a hunt, another was howling for a mate. Some were even providing a warm welcome to a long-lost family member. There was plenty of information flowing through the night air. Listening to the howls of her brothers and aunt, Arnaaluk howled back at them, letting them know where she was. Her beautiful voice resonated across the valley and echoed from the peaks.

For Arnaaluk, howling was more than an instinct. Throughout her life, the wolves in her family had often been far apart. Howling was the method which, even from long distances, brought them closer together. Arnaaluk's howl was an expression of solidarity, and like a mystical force it strengthened the family's domestic bonds. It was a song heard throughout the mountains and forests of the land for countless generations.

To all creatures in range, the howl was a reminder that the wolf was always on the prowl. To the caribou, the wolf's howl was a sound of horror. For thousands of years, the presence of the wolf had kept them moving from one location to another. With every howl, the caribou remained vigilant.

Tulok had never heard Arnaaluk's howl before. It was the loveliest howl he'd ever heard in his life. He responded with a howl of his own, a special howl for Arnaaluk declaring his love for her. His low, deep voice was not strong and beautiful like that of Arnaaluk, and there was a hint of sorrow in his howl. Another howl was heard in reply, the voice of Kanak, asserting *his* love for Arnaaluk. Tulok responded with a confrontational howl at Kanak, and soon the two brothers were howling back and forth, emphasizing their rivalry over her.

Tulok turned his eyes to the north, toward the place of his origin, the home where his family had once lived. He howled for them, but there was no answer. For now, he had given up hope, but Tulok longed for the days of his early life. He had spent his adult life wandering along the banks of the great river - a serene place with rolling hills, trees and the gentle waters of the Yukon. He was comfortable in this area, but he longed to be with those he loved. Without them, his life seemed incomplete. The night landscape did not sound the same without their beautiful and melodious howls.

Although satisfied with her recent catch, Arnaaluk was determined to stay on the trail of the Porcupine herd. She howled again to summon Kiviaq and Nova. They followed her uphill on the other side of the river. Standing on the summit, she sniffed the air and ground for signs of caribou. She howled, requesting help from Tulok, but he did not answer. She searched the nearby valley to no avail and began to worry about him.

After a long wait, Tulok finally answered with another howl. Arnaaluk howled again, summoning him to rejoin the other wolves. She needed his help for the next caribou hunt. The wolves spent days traveling south along the river, tracking the elusive and migratory herds. While Arnaaluk tracked the herd, Tulok howled from time to time to let her know where he was.

Chapter Nineteen

Kanak's Humiliation

As the three wolves set out on their next hunt, Tulok and Kanak found them at the site where they had stopped to rest. Tulok trotted after his brother, sniffing the snow and trees for caribou. Tulok knew he was a better hunter than Kanak and remembered when he witnessed firsthand Kanak's poor skills as a hunter. Kanak had prematurely chased a small herd, disobeying the advice of his father. As a result of his mistake, he, his parents and siblings starved for a time. It was a painful experience for all of them.

The wolves searched the hills, forests and valleys for caribou. Tulok found tracks in the snow and followed them to a small herd gathered in a valley.

"Today, I will prove myself worthy of Arnaaluk's affection. I will prove that I'm not a bad hunter like you think I am." bragged Kanak.

"Go ahead!" Tulok sighed, "I'd like to see you chase down a caribou."

Tulok watched and then followed Kanak as he dashed toward a single doe at the back of the herd. He nipped at her back legs, and then jumped forward, attempting to snag the hindquarters. The doe kicked him in the lower chest, knocking the wind out of him. The kick left him panting and gasping for air.

"Good job!" sneered Tulok.

Kanak lowered his head and tail. Humiliated, he stood before his brother. "Those caribou are hard to catch! I almost caught that doe at the back of the herd!"

Tulok was not impressed. "Well, maybe you need to try harder next time. You'd better watch yourself, Kanak. You wouldn't want a sharp caribou kick to the belly. That happened to me once."

"Really?" asked Kanak.

"That kick got me halfway between the ribs and stomach," Tulok continued. "I was unconscious for a time, then I slumped over and spit up blood for days. I assume a kick that powerful could kill you. Maybe you need some training from me."

"No!" snapped Kanak, "I don't need training from you! I can do it myself!"

"Very well, then," Tulok cynically replied. "Don't expect to be taking down a caribou anytime soon. You don't have the skill. You're not even close to being as tough as I am," he bragged.

While Kanak and Tulok were far behind, Arnaaluk stayed on the chase. No matter how fast she was, she could not catch up with the herd. The caribou, consisting of young and healthy adults, evaded her. The strongest wolf was no match for their speed and agility, and unless one fell or was separated from the herd, they could easily outmaneuver the wolves.

Arnaaluk was out of breath. She panted as she slowed her pace. "Those caribou are too fast for me. I think I've chased the wrong herd."

The herd crossed a hill on the horizon and disappeared. Arnaaluk turned around and slunk back to rejoin the other wolves by the hillside. Once reunited with them, she sighed at Kiviaq, Nova, and Lusa.

"Let's hunt for voles," she said, "We've done the best we can."

Arnaaluk was slightly hungry but not starved. She and her brothers retreated to a deep patch of snow by the trees. They scanned for voles, but there was nothing moving under the snow. She turned to the woods nearby. She searched and sniffed for a snowshoe hare, but none could be found. Returning to the valley along the river, she found Kanak sulking.

"What's the matter?" she asked him.

"I can't catch a caribou. I chased a few but they got away from me."

"I understand that and I'm not surprised. You didn't answer me when I asked you if you were a good hunter…"

"Tulok didn't catch one either," he interrupted, "Besides, he's not the right one for you, Arnaaluk. He is snappy and mean."

"I don't care. He's probably just snappy and mean toward you. Anyway, the truth is, none of us can catch those caribou. They are all healthy adults, too fast for us. Tulok is still quite a hunter."

"Tulok thinks he's the strongest and toughest. He thinks he is superior to me in every way. When we were pups, I frequently abused him into submission. He always let me have whatever I wanted. For a time, he avoided conflicts with me, but soon, he began to dominate me…"

"You abused *him* into submission?" she asked.

Kanak paused for a moment. "Yes, if that's the way you want to put it. I may not be the strongest or the toughest of the litter, but when I was a pup, I controlled my siblings by instilling fear in them."

"Leave me alone!" she snapped.

Arnaaluk put her nose to the ground, sniffing through the snow for signs of the caribou herd that had just evaded her. For now, killing a single caribou on her own was her main objective. It was something she had never done before, and she needed the skill to survive on her own in case something ever happened to her family.

Chapter Twenty

The Caribou That Got Away

Once she finished searching for voles, Arnaaluk yawned and collapsed in the snow. She decided to watch her brothers for a time. First, Nova nipped Kiviaq on the backside, then Kiviaq jumped on top of Nova. Nova rolled over and bared his teeth in surrender. Kiviaq grabbed him by the scruff of the neck and dragged him to Arnaaluk.

Arnaaluk was always eager to play with her brothers. She grabbed Kiviaq's neck and dragged him to the edge of a tall rock. She watched him lose his balance and fall from the rock into the snowbank below. She panted with amusement.

For Arnaaluk, even a moment of play did not erase the pain of a failed hunt. She still groaned about Kanak's lack of skill in hunting caribou, and was skeptical of his abilities to help her family survive. To make matters worse, Tulok was nowhere in sight. Arnaaluk climbed to the top of the tall rock and sulked.

"What's the matter?" asked Kiviaq.

"It's Tulok! He's gone."

For a time, Tulok did not return and she wondered if something had happened to him. Did she drive him away? Was it something she had said? She looked everywhere, waiting for him throughout the day and into the night. She began to assume he would never come back. For now, she didn't care about Tulok's domineering attitude toward his brother, this no longer mattered to her. She was impressed by his hunting skills. She wondered if he had left her, and was seeking another mate.

Arnaaluk stared at the moon, stars, and Aurora Borealis to take her mind off his absence. She got up and ambled to the edge of the river. The same caribou she encountered that afternoon were there, grazing in the snow. Even after two failures she was determined to make a kill on her own.

Now was Arnaaluk's chance to be a strong hunter to the other wolves. She remembered Tulok's words, and tried to recollect everything her father had taught her. Target the weakest in the herd and take no unnecessary risk. Herd the caribou onto difficult terrain. Survey the ground ahead and watch for anything that could cause the herd to stumble - rocks, trees, logs, anything!

She tracked the small herd until they joined with a larger herd along an empty streambed. Arnaaluk knew the right strategy her father used, the same strategy Tulok had reinforced. She surveyed the rocks that littered the ground and examined everything as she crept toward the herd. Not only did she see the herd, but she also began to see the big picture.

Arnaaluk singled out the same doe that Kanak had tried to catch that afternoon. There was something peculiar about her. Her behavior was strange, she was racing and jumping about and her legs were trembling. Saliva was oozing from her mouth. The doe's abnormal behavior led Arnaaluk to suspect she had a disease.

When the doe tried to flee the approaching wolf, she stumbled on the rocks. Arnaaluk leapt forward, seizing the doe's hindquarters, tearing a gaping wound into the perineum.

She then released her jaws from the hindquarters. When the caribou tried to escape, blood gushed and she collapsed. Arnaaluk rushed to the neck and finished her with a bite in the throat. With the doe's last gasp of air, Arnaaluk howled to the other wolves, summoning them to the kill.

Arnaaluk leapt in the air to celebrate the first kill she had made on her own. From her youth, she knew that wolves couldn't always rely on strength through numbers. Sometimes, the strength of an individual was all that mattered.

Arnaaluk waited for an answering howl. Kiviaq was the first to respond, then he, Lusa, and Nova gathered at the carcass, but Tulok was not among them.

The wolves devoured a large chunk of flank and liver. As soon as they had finished eating, Arnaaluk abandoned the doe's carcass for later consumption, if there was any left. She knew the ravens would descend upon the carcass and finish the rest. Regardless of whether ravens, foxes, or bears would finish the carcass, no part of the caribou would ever be wasted.

Chapter Twenty-One

Tulok Returns

While tracking caribou on his own, Tulok paused to listen. Arnaaluk's howl called him, requesting his return. He had a strong temptation to howl back, but then another howl followed, that of Kanak, urging him to go away. Tulok turned his head, assuming Arnaaluk didn't really love him, but he had a strong urge to reconnect with her. A voice in his head told him he belonged with her. If he were to leave her where else could he go? But Kanak's howl caused a stab of remorse – Tulok felt guilty about the way he had treated his brother.

Tulok wandered aimlessly. He paced back and forth along the riverside, foraging in the woodlands, sniffing and turning over every log. He sniffed the spruce, the snow and ground, picking up the scent of a porcupine, but no caribou. For the rest of the day, Tulok searched the rolling hills, but no prey was found.

On a frigid and windy evening, he rejoined Arnaaluk's family at the foot of the hill. He stood before Arnaaluk, her emerald eyes glowing in the night. Overjoyed to see him, Arnaaluk leapt in the air. She kissed him profusely on the left side of his muzzle.

"Tulok! Where have you been?" she asked, "I was worried about you."

"I've been tracking prey."

"Please stay with us. I beg you to stay," she pleaded.

"Why? I don't belong here. I came back to say goodbye."

"What are you talking about? What do you mean?"

Tulok paused for a moment. "Do I have to explain everything to you? When I left home, I never wanted to see Kanak again. I don't want anything to do with him, and I don't want to get in another fight with him. Why do you like me all of a sudden? You don't really need me. Isn't Kanak good enough for you?"

"No, I want nothing to do with him. I don't even like him."

"I'm sorry, Arnaaluk. I don't belong here. If Kanak wants you, I'll let him have you. Don't worry about me."

"Tulok, I need you to stay! My family needs you!"

Tulok saw Kanak approaching. Tulok snarled at him, raising his tail in a horizontal position, ready to fight. Kanak crouched in submission as he had done in times past. He rolled over, exposing his chest and belly, and baring his teeth. Tulok turned around and stalked away, then collapsed in the snow.

Tulok rested his sore and weary body, keeping Arnaaluk in his sight. Seeing the other wolves asleep, nothing else could keep him occupied. For the rest of the night, Tulok curled up in the snow, but could not sleep. A cold wet nose nudged his side, and he turned his head to find Lusa standing by him. He growled at her, preferring to be left alone. Lusa, who was obviously too kind to be deterred by his moodiness, laid down next to him and placed her paw on his shoulder.

"I am here for you, Tulok," she whispered.

"I don't know why I came back," Tulok mumbled, "I don't feel like I belong here."

"Yes, you do belong here. It's your nature to be part of a family."

"I don't know about that. Some other female would suit me, not Arnaaluk."

After growling and sulking for a time, Tulok sighed with resignation, impressed by Lusa's kindness. As a sign of gratitude, he gave her one lick on the side of the neck, rubbed his head on her shoulders, and finally went to sleep.

Although she had been born of a different litter, but of the same parents, Lusa had always been close to Payuk. They had grown up together. She and her brother, Akiak, were devoted to Payuk. When Payuk left home, they joined him on his trek south in search of a mate. She was always close to his offspring and knew all of them very well, even the ones who had left the family.

As she fell asleep, Lusa dreamed of her brother's death. Although she had not witnessed it, she knew how it must have been. Yelping, mauling, biting, the jaws of wolves tearing through flesh and bone, blood spattering through the snow. The horrific sounds echoed through her mind. She dreamed she was deep in the forest all alone. Kiviaq and Nova were not with her. Suddenly, Lycargus emerged from the trees, charging toward her.

The howl of Lycargus roused her from this nightmare. She awoke, gasping in fear. Her eyes darted around her, and although Lycargus was far away, Lusa lived in dread of him. Every night, his howls would fill the air - sometimes close, sometimes further away. Lusa glanced to her right to find Tulok sleeping by her side. She felt safe with him and settled down.

To her, Tulok was a welcome sight. The moment she first saw him, she saw an opportunity to win him as her mate. She was still young and desired to be joined to a mate and bear offspring of her own. She contemplated breaking with the family and running off with Tulok, to raise a family with him.

Early the next morning, Arnaaluk crept into the nearby forest where Tulok was resting in the early sunshine. She rested her head on his chest.

"Arnaaluk! What are you doing here?" asked Tulok.

"I just needed to spend some time with you, Tulok. I want you to know how much I was longing for your return. After all this time waiting, I was beginning to think you were never coming back. I'm not impressed with Kanak's skill in hunting. I'm not impressed with his attitude either." Arnaaluk spoke softly.

"Skill? He doesn't have any. He's so full of himself."

Arnaaluk whimpered over her recent losses. "I remember the times I spent with my uncle, Akiak, and Payuk, my father. They loved me from the day I was born and taught me to hunt and survive. You can teach me, too."

"What more is there to learn?" asked Tulok. "You know everything there is to know about hunting."

As Tulok nuzzled the side of her face, Arnaaluk noticed a change coming over her. From the time she discovered her dead father and uncle, she had developed compassion. Over time, her selfishness had slowly diminished. She sat in the midst of the forest, snuggling up with Tulok. There was something about him that appealed to her.

The scent of caribou carried on the wind interrupted her thoughts. Turning her head toward the north, Arnaaluk opened her eyes and dashed down the hillside, sniffing the air.

"Where are you going?" Tulok asked.

She didn't answer as she studied the snow. She howled then for Tulok and motioned to him. "Come on! More caribou are headed this way!"

Aroused by the howl, Kanak awoke to the scent of caribou. He descended the mountain and rushed through the forest. He hoped he would be able to make the first kill on his own to prove himself superior to his brother. *One caribou kill would impress Arnaaluk*, he reasoned.

Kanak caught up with the herd, but didn't wait for the herd to turn and run. The excited and overconfident wolf darted after them. He made too much noise - the same mistake he'd made previously. He picked up speed until he reached the back of the herd, lunging at their back legs and taking several kicks to the mouth and neck. The sharp hooves left cuts and punctures in his gums. Kanak snapped his jaws toward the legs of the caribou several times, but missed. By this time, the caribou were gone.

Kanak panted. He eyed the caribou escaping over a nearby hill. Blood dripped from the wounds in his mouth and two of his teeth fell out, dropping in the snow. Once again, Kanak lowered his head with shame. The inexperienced wolf collapsed into the snow, tired and stressed. Although he was hungry, the pain for him was not only physical, but also emotional.

Kanak growled, frustrated with his life. He had once lived in a world where he had been dominated by his older brother and parents. Now, having broken with them, he spent time wandering as a lone wolf, looking forward to the day he would find a female. If Tulok stood in his way, Kanak would try to fight him, but he was concerned. Tulok was tenacious and a superior hunter. He was more than an obstacle to Kanak's desires, he was a threat. Kanak realized he had made a serious mistake, by leaving the family before his hunting skills had time to mature. He knew that a wolf must stay with his family to learn hunting and survival, but he had not listened.

Tulok left the other wolves and wandered through the mountains and valleys, searching for caribou. He found their tracks and the marks they left in the forest, but he had no luck finding a herd. Despite his skill, Tulok was now hungry as he had eaten nothing for days.

Tulok yawned and settled into a nap. With an empty stomach and an anxious mind, he found it difficult to sleep. The sound of wolves howling reached his ears. These wolves were preparing for a hunt, but since no caribou were near they were obviously hunting a different type of prey, possibly moose or Dall sheep. Tulok ignored the howls. He knew he could live many days without food. While he was resting, optimism surged within him. He was pleased that Arnaaluk was displaying interest in him.

Chapter Twenty-Two

The True Nature of the Wolf

Just after sunrise on the shortest day of winter, Tulok stood in the center of a dense forest. He watched Arnaaluk paw the snow, hunting for voles. Tulok joined in. He felt the snow for signs of life, then making a vertical leap, he landed on his forepaws. He drew out one vole and tossed it, swallowing it alive. He snatched another vole from the snow and tossed it in the air. Arnaaluk leapt forward and caught it in midair with her teeth. Unimpressed, Tulok stared at Arnaaluk and growled. He did not share her sense of amusement. He was, by this time, familiar with her common trick.

As the day progressed, the two wolves continued to paw the snow, but for now, no more voles could be found.

Arnaaluk returned to the valley where the other wolves gathered. Due to the short winter days, sunrise and sunset were almost back-to-back. She spent the fleeting daylight facing south, basking in the warmth of the sun. She twitched and turned, struggling to keep her eyes closed and her mind empty. As she faded off to sleep, food occupied her thoughts.

Arnaaluk awoke to familiar sounds from a flock of ravens, flying to the west in the evening sky. She followed them to the carcass of a caribou. She howled to the other wolves, alerting them to her discovery. With no other wolves in sight, Arnaaluk went ahead and took the first bite. She started tearing off the caribou's fur piece by piece. First came Tulok's howl, then Kiviaq, Nova, Lusa, and finally Kanak. They were all ready to eat.

Still tired and strained, Kanak trudged downhill toward the carcass. Once he arrived on the scene, he began gnawing on the flank. As the other wolves tore apart the caribou, Kanak was breathing heavily. Not only did starvation and fatigue wear him down, so did fear of his brother.

Tulok stood in front of Kanak, jumping on top of the carcass and growling at him. He nipped at him, warning him to stand back. Kanak snarled and growled in return. Tulok raised the fur on his shoulders and pointed his tail straight back. Kanak appeared nervous, but he did not back away. Tulok snarled and nipped at him, and finally Kanak began to edge backwards. After he had eaten his fill, Tulok left the carcass and returned to his resting spot on the hillside, settling down.

As soon as Tulok was gone, Kanak could do whatever he wanted. He chewed off one of the caribou's legs and devoured the flank, stripping it to the bone. He looked to the sky to find a multitude of ravens. With the ravens picking off large portions of the carcass, Kanak hurriedly devoured the rest. Once he was finished, he lay on the ground, his hunger satisfied.

Tulok watched Kiviaq and Nova playing with each other in the snow, exhausted from the days he had spent tracking caribou and hunting voles. Nevertheless, Tulok stretched his legs and approached the two brothers.

"Tulok!" Kiviaq exclaimed. "You look terrible today! Maybe you need to have fun with us! We've had no time to play with all this hunting and tracking."

Tulok agreed. "I guess you're right!"

With his strong paws, he pushed Nova over and held him down. Nova nipped at Tulok and pushed on his chest, but Tulok stood firm, refusing to budge. Tulok rested his body on Nova, using his weight to keep him restrained, but then released him. Nova ran around to the back of Tulok, nipping him on the tail and challenging him to a game of tag. Tulok chased and tackled him, rolling him on his back, and locked his jaws on the scruff.

Kiviaq then jumped on Tulok's back, trying to tackle him. Tulok wrapped around Kiviaq's neck in a tighter grip, pulling him over until he fell on his side. Reaffirming his physical strength and dominance, Tulok curled his lips, then snarled at him. Kiviaq gave Tulok several licks on the mouth. It was not only a sign of surrender, but a sign of bonding and friendship. Kiviaq then gave him a bear hug around the neck, wrestling the wolf of superior strength. With no resistance, Tulok toppled and rolled over on his back, pretending Kiviaq was the winner of the fight.

After Kiviaq and Nova fell asleep, Tulok wandered into a nearby valley. During the night that followed, he tracked a few caribou. A slight scent touched his nostrils, but in a moment, the scent faded to nothing. Disappointed, Tulok sighed, lowering his head and tail. There were no caribou herds in sight - no tracks, no scent, nothing. Most of the caribou had already gone south.

Tulok returned to the site where the other wolves rested. He watched them from a distance, contemplating leaving them behind. He hoped to find another female somewhere. Maybe he could take Lusa as his mate instead, as she seemed interested in him. Even though there were other options, Tulok yearned for Arnaaluk. A sense of worry regarding their future overcame him. He feared something terrible could happen if he were to abandon these wolves.

As a wolf, Tulok knew a life of loneliness was not healthy for him. He knew his species to be social and he needed to form relationships with other wolves. Tulok knew the values of loyalty and communication, and he considered the sturdy bond he had recently forged with Kiviaq and Nova. Relationships are the foundation for every family unit. It is an adhesive that holds them together, as roots anchoring a tree in the ground. The institution of family and family ties are the foundation upon which wolf society is built. It is the true nature of the wolf.

Tulok, by his instincts, knew how much caribou could feed wolves for a set amount of time. He also knew that the late winter was approaching, and caribou were becoming scarce. For Arnaaluk and her family, one caribou kill would not be enough. Tulok's decision was made - he would stay and become a part of this family.

Chapter Twenty-Three

A Glimmer of Hope in the Dead of Winter

Tulok, now deep in thought, looked to the northwest where dark and ominous clouds loomed over the horizon. A severe winter storm was on its way. The late afternoon sky turned dark, almost black as midnight, and flashes of sheet lightning illuminated the atmosphere above him. The wind picked up, blowing wisps of loose snow across the ground. The winds turned to a gale, unleashing a torrent of blinding snow. Older trees snapped and toppled in the strong winds. For Tulok, the storm raging around him was not a major distraction. For now, there was one thing on his mind – caribou. Tulok traveled farther north through the heavy snow, crossing high mountains. His eyesight was suited for this type of weather and soon, he traveled into a wide gaping valley that looked familiar to him.

Tulok's large paws kept him afloat on layers of fresh snow. He waded into the snowdrifts until the snow was up to his belly, then to his neck. A collapse in the snowdrift, almost buried him. Struggling out of the snow, he climbed back on top and gazed ahead.

To him, this was no ordinary valley. It was a migration route for caribou, a highway that took them north on their journey back to the tundra. He had seen large herds of caribou pass this way. With snow deep enough to slow them, he knew they would be an easy target. Killing one caribou would be easy for him, but to feed the family for the remainder of the winter, more caribou would be needed.

After surveying the valley for a time, Tulok retreated to the middle of the woods at the edge of a mountain. He curled up, shielding his face from the blowing snow with his tail. Tulok knew where the other wolves were and he never feared being lost in a blizzard. This would be unnatural for a wolf. For a time, his best course of action was to wait for a large herd to pass his way. The only question was...how long?

As the storm subsided, Tulok climbed to the summit of the tallest mountain to rejoin his new family. From his position, he watched the valley below and listened for the howls of other wolves, waiting for a message. He listened for one message only - caribou.

Kanak approached Tulok as he sat on the rocky ledge, overlooking the steep mountain.

"Have you found any signs of caribou?" he asked.

"No, but I found one of their migration routes, buried deep in the snow."

Kanak thought Tulok was too sure of himself. "How do you know so much about caribou migration? You seem to have too much confidence in your hunting skills."

"Hunting skills? I learned how to track prey over time. It's a skill I have mastered."

A large family of wolves howled. These were not the same wolves he heard before. Tulok listened to the message their howls conveyed. *Caribou...great in number...coming this way.*

They are traveling to the north, he thought, *through the mountains and into a deep valley*. Tulok didn't know when they would arrive, but he hoped they would arrive soon - in time to keep the wolves from starving.

Over the days that passed, storm after storm swept over the mountain. The wolves rested and waited for the caribou herd to arrive. After much time, Tulok knew the dreadful truth – he had been mistaken. The caribou, for now, were not coming his way after all. They were headed for a different area.

Tulok descended the mountain and searched through the forests, but found no caribou. He snatched voles and hares from time to time, hunting and then resting. After days without sufficient food, he was almost ready to give up hope. His stomach ached with emptiness.

Winter had passed its peak, and for much of the winter there had not been much to eat. During that course of time, the wolves searched everywhere, snatching a hare or two, some voles, or a ptarmigan. Sometimes they would find the bare bones of a caribou. Tulok would lick every trace of blood from the bones or gnaw any flesh hanging from the spine or ribs. After spending many days without large game, Tulok and the other wolves were ready to give up hope.

One morning, the scent of caribou carried on the south wind, reached his nose. He sniffed it in his sleep, then awoke. Following the scent, he found caribou tracks scattered throughout the snow. Tulok howled to alert the others. Arnaaluk, Kanak, Kiviaq, Lusa, and Nova all howled back in unison. They were mobilizing, coming toward the valley on the northeast edge of the river, but Tulok was far ahead of them. The herd was not as large as he had hoped, but with Tulok's eyes set on the caribou, he crept behind a rock, then a tree.

Chapter Twenty-Four

One Caribou Kill, Not Enough

Tulok's legs trembled. He could not wait to descend the hill and pursue the herd. He shifted his sights back and forth, seeking out more than one caribou. One thought dominated his mind - one caribou kill would not be enough. A surplus of caribou must die; four, five, six or more, enough to feed the hungry wolves for the rest of the winter.

Tulok sneaked toward the herd. Taking flight, the caribou thundered down the hillside, descending the tall rocky ledge and fleeing into the valley. The weakest in the herd plowed through the deep snow in a desperate attempt to escape. Tulok bounced through the snow, the other wolves not far behind.

Tulok seized the first caribou in the hindquarters, locking on until the other wolves overwhelmed it. They mauled at the flank, tearing off chunks of flesh as blood gushed. The wolves frantically crawled over its rump and onto its back, biting repeatedly. Leaving this caribou to the other wolves, Tulok raced to the caribou in front of it. As the first, he attacked the flank and hindquarters.

Having incapacitated their first victim, the other wolves besieged the second caribou. Tulok finished it with a bite to the throat. Then, he and Kanak ran after a third caribou. Tulok latched onto the rear, then ran to the front and fixed his jaws on the throat.

The fourth caribou made his way into the shallow snow. Just as it was about to escape, Tulok rushed toward the flank.

Arnaaluk rushed past him and seized the flank with her teeth, pulling on the caribou's hindquarters and dragging it into the deep end of a snowdrift. Tulok and the other wolves joined in and covered its back end with bites.

As the fourth caribou collapsed, Tulok finished it with a fatal bite to the throat. He looked behind him, gazing upon the work he had accomplished. Four caribou now lay dying in the snow.

Kiviaq was overzealous. He ran far ahead of Tulok, chasing the rest of the herd up the hillside. One of them kicked him in the mouth, then gave him a second kick to the neck. Leaping high in the air, Kiviaq aimed his jaws for the back end of a doe. The doe fiercely kicked him in the left side of his chest. A painful crack resounded in one of his ribs. Disoriented and in pain, Kiviaq collapsed. He lay on the ground writhing and coughing up drops of blood in the snow.

Tulok approached him and licked him on the side of the face. "Are you all right?"

"Yes, I'm fine." he wheezed.

Tulok nudged Kiviaq back on his feet.

"I'm alright," Kiviaq rasped, "The pain will go away."

Kiviaq panted as he looked at the four dead caribou lying in the snow. As the wolves prepared to eat, ravens and a few eagles gathered at the kill site.

Tulok nudged Kiviaq toward the carcass, "We haven't got all day, Kiviaq. Let's eat!"

The wolves feasted on the first caribou. When they finished eating, they abandoned the other carcasses for later consumption. Kiviaq was grateful to Tulok for his accomplishment, and he and Nova licked him on the face for the bountiful kills he had made.

The short day came to an end. The sky turned dark as the wolves faded into the woods and a gentle snowfall covered the carcasses and puddles of blood. The caribou remains were hidden from other predators and scavengers for a time.

Tulok, concerned about Kiviaq's pain, lay beside him. As soon as Kiviaq was asleep, Tulok looked to Arnaaluk. She gave him a loving nip on the upper chest and then a lick on the nose for a job well done.

Tulok looked at Kiviaq as he slept in a fetal position. He was breathing heavily, moaning with every breath from the pain of his fractured rib.

"Is he going to be alright?" asked Arnaaluk.

"I don't know," Tulok replied.

Arnaaluk rested her head on the side of her brother's neck. As she fell asleep, Tulok gave her a lick to the muzzle. He retreated to the edge of the hillside and watched the moon and stars, illuminating the night sky.

Chapter Twenty-Five

Devotion of a Wolf

As the other wolves rested, Tulok kept his distance from them. Deep in a nearby forest, he picked up a spruce cone and rolled it through the snow, watching the small snowflakes descending around him. He picked up and tossed a large spruce branch.

Tulok noticed a familiar wolf approaching him. It was Arnaaluk! He dangled the branch in front of her face and she nipped at it, trying to snatch it from him. Remembering the game she played the second time they met, Tulok resisted her every move. This time, Tulok knew not to toss the stick in the air. He recalled the humiliating trick the crafty young wolf had played on him.

Arnaaluk tried to wrestle the stick from his mouth. The stick strained and snapped under pressure. After she dropped her half of the stick, Tulok decided it was time for a gentle fight. Arnaaluk pressed on his side, trying to push him over on the ground, but Tulok placed his paws on her back. She whimpered and crouched before him with respect and licked him on the muzzle.

Arnaaluk abruptly turned and tried to walk away from him, but whimpered, urging him to follow her. Tulok approached her, then stood face to face, gazing into her eyes. Laying his head on the back of her neck, he felt a great compatibility with her.

Wherever she and her family went was where he would go, and whatever happened to them would happen to him. Her family was his family and their trouble was his trouble. If they suffered, he would suffer with them and if they died, he would die with them.

Tulok placed his front paw on Arnaaluk's shoulder. "Earlier this winter, you told me there was something about me that bothered you. Tell me, what is it?" he asked.

"I was concerned about the way you were treating your brother. Kanak told me you bullied and oppressed him when he was young. He also told me you never showed him any love," she replied.

"Kanak treated me the same way when we were pups. He dominated me in fights over meat and bone. By the time he was an adolescent, he was disobedient to our parents. He became arrogant and haughty over time."

"Can't you just reconcile with him?" she asked.

"It's difficult for me to reconcile with him. Kanak is selfish."

Arnaaluk sensed a change overwhelming her. For the first time, she felt a deep affection for another. She could also sense a change in her character. She was no longer as selfish as she had once been. Now was the time to surrender her independence and selfishness, and spend the rest of her life in an inseparable bond with Tulok. In her mind, she envisioned herself assuming the role of a faithful mate. Together, through all their trials, she and Tulok were discovering faithfulness and devotion to each other, part of the wolf's true nature.

Tulok was the wolf she had been seeking - a mate who would give her true love and commitment. This was it! His true character had been revealed to her. He was a strong and skilled hunter of caribou like her father, and unlike Kanak, he had the ability to provide for her family. Tulok was a dominant sibling, much like Arnaaluk, and their personalities attracted each other.

Arnaaluk trotted uphill and returned to the spot where the other wolves were resting.

"That Tulok is a miserable wretch," Kanak remarked, "He thinks he is stronger and a better fighter than I am."

Arnaaluk reminded him of Tulok's strengths. "You must remember Tulok can hunt and kill caribou well. You don't possess his skill."

"So, he's useful to this family. He'll remain with us and hunt caribou to provide for us. He can give his attention to Lusa, Kiviaq or Nova. They're good enough for him, or he could run off with Lusa. She's good enough for any male."

Arnaaluk turned her head away from him. "Why? So you can take me as your mate? Never!"

"I think he should leave."

"No!" she exclaimed, "I won't let him leave. I'm in love with him!"

Kanak suddenly felt insecure. "You don't really love me, do you?"

"No, I don't! Why should I?"

"Arnaaluk! Please!"

"No!"

She turned her nose up and trotted briskly away.

Chapter Twenty-Six

The Confrontation

On a cold and cloudy morning, Kanak knew the time had come. It was time to win Arnaaluk from his dominant brother. There was only one female for him and he knew who it was. Tulok, raising the fur on his back, growled at Kanak, who charged toward him. Tulok snarled and rose to confront his brother. He jutted out his ears and raised his tail. This time, the jealous brother showed no sign of submission.

Kanak stared Tulok in the face. "This all ends today! One of us will be the victor."

Kanak approached Arnaaluk, but she jumped away from him, keeping a safe distance. Kanak gave Tulok a strong bite to the shoulder and he yelped, momentarily backing away. Before long, the two brothers stood face to face, circling each other. They raised the fur on their backs, in preparation for a decisive duel.

"Are you sure you want to do this, Kanak?" said Tulok. "I am more powerful than you."

Kanak stood defiant. "Be careful with me! I can kill you!"

"Well, that's true! You can kill me, but Arnaaluk will never fall for you! She's decided who will be her mate! It's not going to be you!"

"Don't be so sure."

Kanak nipped at Tulok's throat. Tulok briefly jumped away, then seized the fur below Kanak's throat with his teeth. Kanak threw Tulok to the ground and straddled him. Tulok pressed hard against him and pushed him off, getting back on his feet. Kanak mauled him viciously, covering his neck and left shoulder with bite wounds, and sinking his teeth into Tulok's foreleg, Kanak tried to break the bone. Tulok jerked away, but Kanak seized Tulok by the side of the neck, dragging him through the snow.

For a moment, the snarling, biting, and yelping ceased. The two wolves paused to catch their breaths, and then the snarling and growling resumed. Kanak seized Tulok's neck with a powerful bite, hurling him to the ground. Tulok tried to keep him off by pressing against his chest, and finally, Tulok reached forward and seized Kanak by the scruff of the neck. Getting back to his feet, Tulok flipped Kanak on his side, then pressed him to the ground with his paws.

For a moment, Tulok believed he had won the fight against his brother, but he was wrong. Kanak counterattacked. He bear-hugged Tulok around the neck, but Tulok's legs stood firm. Pressing Kanak on the shoulders, Tulok hurled him to the ground and pinned him into the snow. Tulok stood towering over Kanak, his lips curled with disdain. Making one last attempt to fight back, Kanak struggled with all his might. Tulok pressed even harder, and with a final snarl, he placed his teeth near Kanak's neck.

Kanak rolled over on his back, exposing his chest and belly to Tulok. He whimpered, urging Tulok to refrain from any more aggression. After Kanak rose shakily to his feet, Tulok circled his defeated brother.

"You will live by my rules," Tulok growled. "I'm your older brother and Arnaaluk is mine. Do you understand?"

Approaching Arnaaluk from the side, Tulok stood next to her. She rubbed against his chest and he traced his muzzle across her fur. Tulok turned to look at Kanak. For the rest of the day and into the evening, Tulok circled Arnaaluk, guarding his mate. He raised his neck and tail to full posture as a flag raised to full mast.

After several days, as a sign of reconciliation, Kanak received a lick on the muzzle from Tulok. Kanak placed his head on Tulok's chest, and then crouched before his brother. He rested in the snow, admitting defeat. As a sign of victory over him, Tulok howled loudly, with Arnaaluk joining him.

Kanak settled on a ledge overlooking the valley below. It was over for him. For many seasons, he had wandered along these lands in search of a mate. Now he was humiliated before his brother. He had long been the underdog of a sibling rivalry, and nothing would ever change. He sighed, having lost the chance to win Arnaaluk, crushed under the weight of his brother's victory. Now he cowered under the eye of Tulok, who was watching him from the mountain summit.

Chapter Twenty-Seven

Tulok's Nightmare

Many days passed. One evening, Tulok cuddled up with Arnaaluk on the banks of the frozen river, keeping their distance from the other wolves. Tulok and Arnaaluk were both sleepy, but remained awake, watching the reflection of the moon shining across the ice. Tulok placed his paw on Arnaaluk's shoulder and touched his nose to hers. As the Aurora Borealis flashed its stunning colors before their eyes, Tulok instinctively knew why he was here and had come this far. He yearned to not to just start a family, but to be a part of one.

"Are you still awake?" Tulok asked Arnaaluk.

"Yes, barely," she mumbled. "I am so happy to have you as my mate. I have hope for our future."

Tulok took time to savor the moment. He watched a shooting star streaking across the night sky.

Tulok's mind faded to a dream. An image appeared of Arnaaluk wandering through the forest. Suddenly there was a loud click. A tall figure appeared before her and then there was a loud bang. Tulok ran to investigate, finding her lying on the ground writhing in pain, nipping at her side. Seeing one of those tall dreaded figures approaching, Tulok turned and ran, leaving her behind. Another bang rattled the air.

He turned to look back, but she was gone. There was nothing left but a puddle of blood and pieces of fur scattered across the snow. Tulok howled in mourning, then laid his body on the spot where Arnaaluk had met her end. With no female, he would have no pups so the future of his family was now in jeopardy.

Tulok turned to see the other wolves wandering and howling in bereavement. Suddenly there was a loud snap, as a pair of metallic jaws caught him around his front paw. As he struggled to free himself, he heard footsteps approaching. A click sounded, then a bang and everything went dark.

Tulok looked down upon the other wolves, as if he were an invisible, ghostly figure. With the two wolves they relied on for hunting caribou gone, the other wolves grew gaunt and weak. They chased caribou but could not catch one. First to collapse was Kanak, falling on his side and writhing in agony with the pain of hunger. During Kanak's last breaths, Tulok drifted to his starved body.

Tulok looked in the eyes of his dying brother, then looked up to find the other wolves scattered across the nearby valley, dead before him. Before his eyes, they decomposed and turned to bones. The land fell silent and not a howl could be heard.

Tulok awoke from his sleep, breathing heavily and shaking with fear. His mind was haunted by the tall beings who moved through the forest. He was relieved to find Arnaaluk sleeping next to him, and the other wolves resting in the distance. All of them were sound asleep, alive and well. Tulok feared something horrific was moving through the mountains and forests. Tall creatures carrying sticks that made loud noises, able to fire sharp, hot objects into any living thing. Tall creatures that killed predator and prey alike, and did not value wolves as families or individuals. This was a recurring nightmare Tulok had experienced several times recently. *Was it becoming a grim omen?* He wondered.

Tulok placed his paw on Arnaaluk's shoulder. With the sight of seeing her alive, his nerves calmed. His mind slowly reeled from the nightmare he just had.

"What's going on?" she mumbled.

"I've had a nightmare."

"A nightmare? Why do you awaken me for a nightmare?"

"Arnaaluk, it's serious! Something terrible is going to happen!"

"How do you know? It was just a dream!"

"It's that same nightmare! Those dreaded tall figures carrying large sticks that go bang!"

"Oh! Yes! I've heard about them! Well, I've never seen one! I don't even know if they exist. They're probably just old tales our ancestors told us."

"They are real! I've seen one! You must believe me!"

"Tulok, do me a favor. Go back to sleep and dream of something else. I think you've been seeing things."

Tulok looked around him, watching for shadows moving among the trees. Seeing no sign of danger, he closed his eyes and went back to sleep. He was puzzled that Arnaaluk disbelieved him and worried for her. He knew that sooner or later the truth would be revealed – that those tall figures were real. This was not just a nightmare, it was a warning.

Chapter Twenty-Eight

The Predator Becomes the Prey

Just before sunrise the next morning, Arnaaluk rose and descended the mountainside. She trotted briefly through the nearby forest. Everything was peaceful and serene, there was nothing to fear. There was no sound except for an occasional breeze, the plop of loose snow falling from a tree branch, and the calls of ravens.

"Tulok thinks something's out to get us," she murmured, "Silly goose!"

She looked ahead. There was something strange and shadowy in front of her - the silhouette of a tall, standing figure. Arnaaluk paused with curiosity and stood still. The figure moved and she quickly took a few steps back. The figure raised a large object like a stick and pointed it directly at her. Then came a loud click. Arnaaluk's curiosity turned to fear, shock flowing through her. In a moment, all her skepticism had vanished. This was a tall figure carrying a stick! Her father's warnings were right! Her instincts told her to flee.

Arnaaluk jolted, turned and ran. Bang! A patch of snow exploded right next to her. She kept running, dashing as fast as she could. Another loud bang and something hot grazed her fur. Falling over, she jumped up and ran even faster. The words of her father flashed through her mind - a warning of metallic teeth that emerged from the ground, grabbing a hapless victim. Loud sticks that went bang sending hot projectiles into their targets. This was not just a tale! This was real! Tulok's fears and nightmares had been justified.

Tulok was asleep on the mountainside when heard the loud bang. Jumping in shock, he rushed toward the sound, then sniffed the air. A strange sulfurous scent entered his nostrils, filling him with dread. Keeping his eyes on Arnaaluk's tracks, he rushed into the nearby forest, fearing his nightmare had come true. Was Arnaaluk's body lying in the snow in a pool of blood? Could she have escaped? If only she had listened!

"No!" Tulok whispered. "They've killed her!"

Tulok feared the worst as his heart beat wildly. This was a sound he had heard before, the sound of death. He rushed deep into the forest, the scent of gunpowder mingled with that of Arnaaluk. With every step he took, Tulok trembled with the thought of finding her dead. Pausing to catch his breath, the forest was silent. Tulok didn't want to follow her tracks any further, dreading what he would find.

He stood silent and paused to listen. Then came the sound of footsteps dashing toward him. At first, he thought it was the figure carrying a gun, but suddenly, another wolf raced from the trees. It was Arnaaluk!

"Something is after me!" she exclaimed.

Tulok licked her on the side of the neck to comfort her. "I know! You had me so worried! I thought you were gone forever!"

Tulok paused to listen again, but he heard nothing behind Arnaaluk. He knew if she had been killed, she could no longer provide for her family and this would be disastrous. With danger stalking the nearby forest, he knew he and the other wolves needed to hide.

Tulok howled to alert the other wolves. Heeding his warning, they abandoned their resting spot and retreated into a dense forest at the edge of the mountain. They remained there for the rest of the day.

As the short day drew to a close, the wolves emerged into the open. They were aware most of these figures never roamed at night. Tulok huddled with Arnaaluk, constantly looking in every direction, paranoid and fearful. He listened attentively for another bang, but none were heard.

Tulok entered the nearby forest and descended into the valley where he and the other wolves had killed four caribou. No carcass was in sight and there was nothing but unusual oval-shaped tracks. He smelled strange scents at the scene, and the carcasses of the remaining caribou the wolves killed had disappeared.

Chapter Twenty-Nine

The Time of Vengeance Has Come

A long span of time passed after Arnaaluk's scare. Soon, it was almost a distant memory. Arnaaluk and Nova were tracking caribou along the northeast bend of the river. Nova foraged the ground further inland, when a wolf's scent crossed his nose. It was a scent he had become familiar with, the dreaded stench of Lycargus. He heard padding footsteps approaching, then, came a growl. Nova quickly looked up to see a larger wolf snarling at him. He whimpered for his sister, but she was nowhere in sight. The large, menacing wolf stared at him, coming closer to sniff his fur.

Nova crouched before him and bared his teeth to appease the strange wolf. He knew this wolf was Lycargus, his greatest fear.

"How foolish of you to cross paths with me. Do you not know whose territory you've just infringed upon?" Lycargus snarled.

Nova did not answer.

"Are you afraid to answer?" Lycargus growled, "Yes! You are afraid! I see you cringe before me."

Lycargus paused to sniff Nova's fur. This was the scent belonging to the family of Payuk, whom he hated and scorned.

"Payuk! The bloodline of Payuk! Now is another chance to avenge the blood of my father!" he growled.

"Please!" Nova pleaded! "Don't kill me! There are very few of us left..."

"So, some of them are still alive?" Lycargus interrupted, "The ones who escaped my clutches. Lusa, Kiviaq, and...Arnaaluk! Where are they?"

"I don't know."

"Well, I know where you are! Don't try to run from me. I will chase you down and rip you to shreds. I will tear apart your flesh and feed you to the ravens, just like I did to your father!"

Arnaaluk came across the scent of Lycargus at the border of his territory. Seeing the tracks of her brother, she dashed up the mountainside into the dense forest following Nova's trail. To her horror, she found the tracks of Lycargus littered across the snow. There she found him - by a den, standing face to face with her brother. Slipping back and hiding in a nearby thicket, she was aware her scent could give her away. Finding an area where the scent of caribou was strong, she rolled in the scent, trying to conceal herself. For a time, she felt safe.

An urge to confront Lycargus overwhelmed her. She did not want her brother torn to shreds, suffering the same fate as her father. She crouched in the thicket and curled her lips, preparing to fight if the time should come. She could not hide forever, and sooner or later, she would have to leave the site and return to her own territory. Staying there would warrant certain death.

It was too late. Arnaaluk's scent distracted Lycargus. "What's that? I smell someone familiar!"

Amak and two of Lycargus' sons were guarding the nearby den and Lycargus motioned to them. They descended the hillside and surrounded Nova.

"Keep an eye on him. Don't let him escape!" Lycargus commanded them.

Sniffing among the trees, he whispered for her, "I know you're out there. I can smell you from over here. Don't be afraid! Come out and show yourself to me! There's no need to hide!"

Lycargus knew who it was. He had often followed her scent. Finding her tracks in the snow, he rubbed his nose in each track. "I know it's you, Arnaaluk. You were lucky to have escaped me twice. Now your days of running and hiding are over. Come out and face me, you coward!"

He stood outside the thicket. "I see you in there. Now come out and face me! Come out and face me if you're a big girl! Come out and face me if you're not a coward!"

Arnaaluk emerged from her hiding place. Lycargus panted and licked his gums. "There you are!"

Strangely, this time Arnaaluk was not afraid of him. She did not tremble in fear, nor did she crouch. She stood staring at him. "I knew I smelled a vile stench emanating from your territory," she growled.

She made her way down the mountainside and stood in front of Nova, guarding him.

Lycargus curled his lips at her, showing his strong teeth and raised the fur on his back. "Arnaaluk! It's pleasant of you to join us to witness the death of your brother or should I say…the death of you both!"

Arnaaluk stood defiant. His snarling did not intimidate her and she did not back down, nor run from him.

"What? Are you not afraid of me?" Lycargus growled.

Arnaaluk, feeling a new sense of courage, stared at Lycargus and the other wolves. "I fear no one!"

"No! You are afraid of me!" Lycargus sneered, "You are very afraid of me! I am your worst nightmare! Now tell me, why are you here? Why did you intrude into my domain?"

"You are threatening my brother."

"Yes, I am threatening your brother. Do I care that he's your brother? Do you have any remorse for *my* brothers? The ones who I watched suffer and die when I was young? Do you have any remorse for *my* father? The one who was killed by Alootook?"

"I don't know what you're talking about," she snapped.

"Alootook was your grandfather, I assume your father never told you about him."

"I did hear about him. I didn't know he killed your father."

Lycargus sniffed her fur, "Tulok! You took him as your mate, didn't you? This is perfect! Now I have a chance to put an end to you and your wretched bloodline. I will trace your steps all the way back to where your family is gathered. Once I find them, I will kill them all - Lusa, Kiviaq and Tulok. Their lives will be over!"

Lycargus continued, "This day will be remembered forever. It is a day of vengeance! The opportunity to rob your family of their offspring and provider. This will be the end of what is left of Payuk!"

Arnaaluk raised the fur on her back, confronting him. "There are just five of us, and how many in your family?"

"Only nine, plus five pups, born yesterday. Many of us have starved through the winter, but soon we will be strong and unstoppable! We may be few, but you are fewer! You and your family are slowly dying out. What you did to my father and siblings, I will do to your bloodline, daughter of Payuk. I will leave your family the way you left mine - crippled and broken!"

To Lycargus, vengeance was truly his. He now had a chance to destroy whatever remained of his rivals. "The end has come for you, Arnaaluk!"

"Run!" Nova whispered to her, "Please run and leave me behind. You are important to the family. Just go!"

"No!" she answered, "I will die for my brother! Future generations of us will remember me."

135

"There will be no future generations!" Lycargus snarled. "Your family will be gone by tomorrow morning. I swear, as the sun rises and sets, I shall kill you all."

Arnaaluk jumped toward Lycargus, nipping him on the shoulder. She locked her forelegs onto his neck and hurled him to the ground, as Lycargus slashed the fur on her back with his teeth. Arnaaluk tried to fight back, but the other wolves overwhelmed her. Their bite wounds covered her shoulders and sides. Lycargus grabbed Arnaaluk by the scruff of her neck and dragged her through the snow with his lips curled and his teeth next to her throat.

Nova ran behind Lycargus and nipped him on the backside. Lycargus turned from Arnaaluk and jumped on Nova, mauling him viciously. Nova squeezed out from beneath him, scurrying as Lycargus and the wolves chased him through the snow. Nova tripped and fell, and the enemy wolves grabbed him by the neck, tackling him to the ground like a caribou.

Teeth were ripping through his fur and skin, and blood was streaming down his throat. Nova feared this was the end. He decided there was only one way to survive - to pretend he was dead. He held his breath and lay with his eyes closed and his mouth open.

Amak nudged him. "He looks dead to me."

Lycargus nudged him as well. "I think you're right, but let's make sure."

Suddenly, they jumped at the sound of a gunshot.

136

"Killers!" shouted Amak, "I just heard a loud bang!"

"Go back and check the den!" shouted Lycargus. "Arnaaluk and Nova are already dead. I will deal with the rest of Payuk's family!"

The other wolves ran away leaving Nova lying in the snow. Hearing another gunshot, Nova opened his eyes, looking around him. All the wolves surrounding him were gone. Slowly, Nova lifted his body from the ground and limped toward the edge of the forest, sniffing the marked territory. He crept over the border and continued on his way. Finding Arnaaluk's fresh tracks and scent in the snow, he knew she had also escaped from Lycargus. As he ran through the forest, Nova watched for tall figures with sticks.

As day turned to evening, Lycargus rushed through the forest. He retraced Arnaaluk's steps, scrutinizing every track. Picking up her scent and following it toward the edge of the forest, he paused. The wind carried more scents - the scents of Lusa, Kiviaq, Kanak and Tulok. Lycargus panted with anticipation. Now that Arnaaluk and Nova were gone, or so he thought, the demise of the rival wolves was now within reach.

Footsteps interrupted his thoughts. Lycargus turned his head to find a tall figure standing near him. A loud click sounded. Bang! Melting into the snow in a pool of blood, Lycargus breathed an agonal sigh.

Chapter Thirty

The Demise of Lycargus

Alasie, the mate of Lycargus, had left her pups to search for food when she heard the loud bang. It was a sound of death. She rushed down the hillside following Lycargus' scent, frantically looking for him. She paused in front of two trees and froze with shock at a sulfurous scent. As she passed between the trees, a snare closed around her neck. Struggling and thrashing, she fought for her life.

She finally stood still. What about the pups back at the den? What about Lycargus? She pulled and wrenched trying to free herself, but the wires constricted her veins and cut off her circulation. She remained in the trap for the entire day and into the evening.

As she struggled, the powerful muscles in her neck contracted as blood rushed to her head. Her ears became clogged, so she could barely hear and soon, she lost consciousness and everything went dark. It was a slow and agonal death.

The gunshot awoke Tulok from his sleep. Rushing into the nearby forest, he found Arnaaluk badly wounded and bleeding. She collapsed in the snow before him. Tulok sniffed and examined her fur, but these were not gunshot wounds, these were bite wounds. He picked her up by the scruff of her neck and began dragging her back to the site where her family was anxiously waiting.

Arnaaluk, using her remaining strength, picked herself up. "It's okay, Tulok! I'll be alright!" She hobbled back to the summit of the hill where her family rushed toward her.

Tulok followed Lycargus' scent into the middle of the forest. He followed the tracks in the snow until the scent of sulfur entered his nostrils. There he found drops of blood and pieces of fur. Lycargus was gone. The enemy of Arnaaluk and her family had been vanquished, but this was no victory for them. For a time, there was silence, but it was soon broken by eerie, mournful howls.

"Lycargus!" Tulok whispered.

Tulok now understood that Lycargus was not the greatest enemy he faced. He knew there was a greater enemy - it was an enemy that could eradicate his entire family, as well as their species.

Bang! Another gunshot reached his ears as fear flowed through him. Fearing for his family, Tulok turned and rushed toward the open valley where he found Arnaaluk and the other wolves safe. Nova had also returned and Lusa was licking their wounds. Kanak was standing vigilant on a nearby hillside. From a distance, Tulok listened to the mournful howls of those in Lycargus' family.

Rising with anxiety, Tulok trotted away from the others, sniffing and searching through the forest. He sniffed the

139

marked territory of Lycargus. Gazing far ahead, he saw a wolf hanging between two trees. Although he was hesitant to enter their territory, he approached the scene and gasped at the grisly sight. A young female wolf was hanging between two trees, strangled, her eyes bulging and a look of anguish and fear on her face.

Shock jolted him once again. This was nothing he had ever seen before. He sniffed her to discover she was part of Lycargus' family, possibly one of his sisters or his mate. Backing away from the scene, fear overwhelmed him. He wondered if this snare could come to life and kill him, too.

Traumatized, Tulok raced uphill through the forest. He frantically watched the ground, wary of steel teeth and strong wires in between trees. On the summit by the den, he found Lycargus' family in silence. Then, the silence was broken by mournful howls. Tulok cautiously stood by the den. Although he was near, the other wolves ignored him, and they did not attack. Tulok stopped to gaze inside and saw Alasie's pups crawling around, unable to leave the den. Tulok felt tempted to howl to Arnaaluk and the others, summoning them. He and Arnaaluk's family could raise these pups together. Then, suddenly came the sound of footsteps. Sensing their approach, Tulok quickly ducked behind a tree.

By instinct, Tulok had learned to fear and avoid these tall figures that roamed in the woods. He learned to avoid their traps and guns. Tulok watched from a safe distance, as the wolves guarding the den fled.

As the pups wandered in the den without their mother, the figure stood outside the entrance. He threw a canister inside, which hit the rocks and ruptured. A mist engulfed the den, which burned the eyes and lungs of the pups. Their whimpers turned to shrieks of agony.

Tulok could hear the pups shrieking in pain - it was a shrill, hideous sound. Once the tall figure had left the den, Tulok rushed toward its entrance. The mist was dense and foggy, but Tulok poked his head into the den in an attempt to rescue the pups. The mist burned his eyes so he could not see. Withdrawing his head and staggering back, tears streamed down Tulok's eyes and muzzle. Coughing violently, he tried to clear his throat of the noxious gas.

Tulok's adrenaline flowed. Never in his life had Tulok witnessed anything so horrible or brutal. When the shrieking died down, he stood in shock. His life would never be the same after what he had witnessed in the den.

Tulok descended the mountainside to rejoin his family. While he dashed through the forest, the shrieks from the pups vibrated in his ears. Five short lives ended with no chance to see the world. Not a chance to open their eyes, to play, socialize or hunt.

Chapter Thirty-One

Home Again

Arnaaluk healed slowly over the next few days. She frequently looked at the nearby hill, where Lycargus, his mate, and their pups had met their violent ends. It was also the same hill where her father Payuk had met his fate last autumn. She climbed the north side of the hill, and once on the summit, found complete silence. There was no trace of marked territory from the enemy wolves, they had all fled. There was no gunpowder scent and no traps. Everything seemed safe.

Arnaaluk surveyed the landscape. This was a world she had not ventured into since last autumn. She saw many landmarks that were familiar to her - the large boulder and trees that she and her family had rested among. She climbed to the top of the boulder and gazed over the land where she had once lived. To her, this was more than an ordinary hill - this place was her home. Like every other wolf, she had an emotional connection to her territory, and she longed to return. Overwhelmed with joy, she howled for the others to join her.

Tulok, the first to arrive, climbed to the boulder and sat next to her. She licked the side of his face with affection and gratitude and laid her paw upon his back, pressing next to him with a bond of love and closeness.

Arnaaluk looked down on the place where her father had been killed. Nothing remained of him but a few bones sticking out of the snow. Still haunted by memories of his death, Arnaaluk climbed down and approached the dried bones, sniffing them. She was overcome by a sudden outpouring of grief. The image of him torn to pieces flashed through her mind.

"This is the spot where he was killed! This is all that remains of him." she cried.

"Who?" Tulok asked.

"Payuk! My father!"

A loud coughing interrupted her time of mourning. She ran to the other side of the large boulder where she found Kiviaq.

"Kiviaq, what's wrong?" she whimpered, "You've been coughing ever since that caribou kicked you in the chest."

"My chest hurts! I can't breathe like I used to. The pain is growing worse every day!"

Arnaaluk laid next to him, placing her paw on his back. "Oh, Kiviaq! Don't make me worry! You'll be better soon, I hope." She licked him across the side of the head.

During the evening, she sat by his side. She instinctively knew he was weak and sick. For now, she was optimistic about his recovery, but that optimism would slowly fade away.

Chapter Thirty-Two

Changing Times

As the winter passed, Tulok looked for opportunities to restore the bond with his brother, Kanak. Finding a branch lying on the ground, Tulok grabbed it with his teeth and dangled it in front of Kanak, teasing him. Kanak grabbed the branch and tried to pry it from his jaws. Tulok jumped onto his back.

"You really need to be re-trained!" he joked, "You must have forgotten how to fight a stronger wolf...like me!"

He pushed Kanak over on his side, placing his paws on his back and pinning him to the ground. As Tulok teased him a second time, Kanak snatched the branch and tugged at it. Tulok released the branch and ran behind Kanak. Nipping him on the tail, he took off running as Kanak chased him down the hillside. Tulok slowed his pace so Kanak could catch up with him. As a sign of reconciliation with his brother, Tulok rolled over on his back. He pretended Kanak was the victor.

"Now you've won, she's yours!"

"Really?" asked Kanak.

"No! We're just pretending! Arnaaluk is still mine!"

By the time they finished playing, Kanak licked Tulok on the muzzle to settle their differences. Tulok, in return, gave

Kanak a lick on the side of the neck. As brothers, they once again walked shoulder to shoulder, wagging their tails. Tulok came to rest next to Arnaaluk, with Kanak huddling next to him. The three wolves relaxed together, watching the sunset and napping from time to time. Nevertheless, for Kanak and Tulok, it would be an uneasy peace.

After a short nap early that night, Arnaaluk awoke. She stretched her legs and took a deep breath, refreshed with hope for herself and those close to her. With the enemy wolves gone, she spent time resting on the banks of the river. She noticed something different - a maternal sensation flowing through her. She had never felt this way before. During the night, she looked for a den by the river, remembering what Tulok said on their second encounter, "Were you born in that den I passed by the river this morning?"

Then, right before her, there it was! A small den with an entrance wide enough for her to squeeze through. Finding the den empty, she crept inside and laid on the cold soft floor, warming it with her body. Draping her tail over her paws, she took a deep breath and rested her head on the floor.

Meanwhile, Tulok along with the other wolves, chased a small caribou herd toward the icy river. As the herd crossed, Tulok lunged at the hindquarters of a single bull, receiving a kick to the shoulder, which caused him to slip and fall on the ice. He got back up, but then stepped on a weak spot. The ice cracked beneath him and he fell through, plunging into the water with a splash.

Tulok emerged from the frigid water and crawled back on top of the ice shaking the water from his fur. When he turned his head toward the caribou, he could see them staring at him. Humiliated, Tulok crouched before the herd and snarled at them.

"What are you looking at?" he mumbled. He cantered toward them until they turned and ran.

Once the caribou had fled, Tulok limped back to shore. He rested his tender shoulder in the snow beside the den and turned to find Arnaaluk crawling inside. He approached her as she lay on the floor.

He poked his head through the entrance. "Arnaaluk, what are you doing in there?"

"What does it look like I'm doing? I'm resting! Don't you remember? This is the den you told me about! You asked if I was born here."

"Yes! I do remember. I know what you mean. Is it for a litter of pups?"

Arnaaluk nodded. "It is as you say."

As a sign of submission and respect, Tulok backed away from the den, crouching before his mate. She now held dominance over him and for a time, he would feed, spoil, and guard her. Shortly after Arnaaluk's announcement, Tulok made the first howl. With the declaration came great joy flowing through the other wolves and they howled together in solidarity not once, but twice.

Tulok had much joy over the change about to take place, but he was also dismayed over the lack of a caribou kill that day. Nevertheless, a feeling of responsibility came over him - the responsibility of caring not only for his mate, but also a family. A new challenge awaited him.

Chapter Thirty-Three

A Tragic Farewell

As Tulok waited by the den where Arnaaluk nested, Kanak approached him and playfully bit him on the scruff. Tulok did not respond.

"Tulok!" Kanak whimpered, "What's wrong? You seem so quiet."

Tulok sighed. "Things have changed so fast. I remember being a young pup, and the times I used to scuffle with you. Now, I'm an adult, and I have pups of my own, not yet born. I now have everything I want, and there is nothing else to fight for. You are born, you mature, you grow old, then you die and become food for the ravens. Our family has been gone a long time, and you and I are the only ones left. Winning Arnaaluk as my mate will not bring them back."

"When did you last see them?" asked Kanak.

"You're not going to like it."

"What do you mean?"

"Our mother died just before I left home. A strange creature on the forest floor snapped around her paw. It was strong as a rock and had teeth like a wolverine. She was caught for two days, then a killer approached her and shot her. Our family could not survive without her hunting skills. I didn't want to tell you at first."

Kanak paused. "What! You never told me!"

Tulok continued, "Our family was starving. They had not only lost a mother, but a provider. As wolves, we need our elders to help us learn to hunt and survive. Our elders pass their knowledge from one generation to the next. Our two younger siblings didn't learn any of this, and they didn't have the skill to survive on their own. There's little hope they could have lasted this long."

"Our father could've cared for them. What about our father?" asked Kanak.

Kanak's and Tulok's mother had been an excellent hunter and provider for the other wolves, and much of her skill had been passed down to Tulok.

On a snowy morning, their father, Mammak had been searching for food in the rolling hills along the river. Tulok found him feeding on the carcass of a caribou lying in the snow. That's when everything changed. Suddenly, his father toppled. He trembled with anxiety, although there was no danger. He lay on the ground breathing heavily.

"Father, what's wrong?" asked Tulok.

"I don't know!" he moaned.

The confused old wolf scampered in every direction, until he was exhausted and out of breath, then collapsed in the snow. Tulok stood over him, whimpering with concern as Mammak jerked with a painful muscle contraction in his shoulder and another spasm wrenched his back. His entire body trembled, his legs stiffened and his neck and back curved into an arch. His jaws tightened and Tulok could tell he was trapped in the grip of severe pain. At first, Mammak whimpered, then his whimpers turned to yelps. The yelps amplified until they became deafening, hideous screams.

Tulok was helpless. He stared in shock, watching his father paralyzed on the ground. The sounds were so heart-wrenching that Tulok backed away. He was unable to bear the shock and trauma of what was playing out before his eyes. Finally, the screams died down as the old wolf struggled to breathe. He lay suffocating with paralysis and then, he breathed his last.

Tulok nudged his father but he did not move. He rushed toward the caribou carcass, sniffing it, only to find an unusual scent. It was a smell he would learn to fear, a substance that could kill any animal. Not only was his father poisoned, but there were also dead ravens and a dead fox lying next to the caribou.

As soon as he recovered from the shock of his father's death, Tulok howled for him. With his siblings still in mourning for their mother, the grief was too much. Tulok approached his two remaining siblings. He kissed them on the muzzles and rubbed his head against their necks and backs. Then, a deep hesitancy gripped his heart and guilt flooded his mind. He felt uneasy about leaving these two untrained siblings on their own as he feared they would die of starvation without him, but Tulok had no choice. If he left and tried to survive in the wild alone, he would probably die but he had to leave. He had to seek a mate. He whimpered at them, begging them to join him, but they would not. His eyes grew misty as he departed. Turning his head to take one last look at the mountains, the land his family called home, Tulok sadly trotted away. As he wandered along the rolling hills by the river, he never forgot about them. He howled for them, but no answer ever came.

Tulok finished his story. "Our parents are gone and there's little hope that our last two siblings are still alive. I howl for them every day. I haven't given up hope."

"Why didn't you tell me, Tulok? Why didn't you tell me they were dead?"

"I didn't want to hurt you. I didn't want to tell you."

Kanak descended the slope outside the den, trembling with grief and rage.

Chapter Thirty-Four

Goodbye, My Brother

Tulok spent two days at rest, then summoned the other wolves with a howl. The hungry wolves followed him to look for caribou, until they reached a mountainside overlooking the river. Tulok climbed to the summit and rested his legs, paws, and aching shoulder in the snow. He gazed on the open valley, but saw no caribou. There were no tracks or scent.

After a few moments of rest, the wolves descended the mountain, single file. Tulok traveled farther to the northwest and trekked several miles searching for scent and tracks. Something smelled familiar and he paused and sniffed the air. Caribou!

Tulok turned northeast and crossed another mountain. He gazed far into the distance and spotted three caribou grazing below him. The caribou were so far away they were tiny specks, but Tulok studied their shape with his excellent vision. He stood watching them, then descended the hillside quietly.

Tulok chased the caribou prematurely and made too much noise. After only a moment, they were out of his reach. It was a terrible mistake and Tulok slowed to a trot, then halted and stood still. Panting, he watched the caribou flee over the mountain on the horizon. Once the caribou escaped to a safe distance, Tulok sighed and his head and tail drooped with dismay. Tulok knew if he or the other wolves failed to find food, Arnaaluk would starve and her unborn pups would be lost. It would be a heart-wrenching loss for all of them.

Kanak, still grieved over learning of the loss of his parents, gave Tulok a stare of disapproval. "Good job! You really know how to hunt caribou," he uttered, "I'm not happy with you taking Arnaaluk from me. You've robbed me of what is mine."

Tulok growled back. "Yours? She wanted me instead of you."

Kanak lowered his tail and hunched over in a confronting pose. "I came here so I could be with her and win her as mate."

Tulok placed his head on Kanak's neck. "And you lost her!"

Kanak felt resentment growing toward his brother. "So be it! If this is the way you want things to be, then I never belonged here."

Turning and trotting away from Tulok, Kanak glanced back at his brother. "Go back to the den! I'm leaving!"

"Kanak, you can't do this!"

"I said go back to the den! I'm through with you!" Kanak snarled.

"So...where are you going? To reunite with our old family?"

"Yes, I'd rather be with them. I'll find them somewhere."

"Fine! Go ahead!" Tulok growled, "Have it your way! Be on your own! I'm not stopping you."

Tulok gazed at him until he vanished over the horizon to the north. Sadness enveloped him as he realized Kanak was gone and would probably not survive on his own. In a way, he was also happy to see him leave. He now had Arnaaluk and the other wolves all to himself. All the times he had spent with Kanak flashed through his mind. The harsh memories of the rivalry with his brother resonated with Tulok the most.

Tulok retreated into the forest where he searched for food. Having no luck, he returned to the den at the riverside. He rested his head on a mound of earth and listened to the cracking of the ice as it expanded and thawed. Turning his gaze to the twilight sky, Tulok listened to the howls of other wolves across the river. He lifted his head hoping it was his own family, but when he listened again, he knew it was not.

Arnaaluk crept out of her den and approached Tulok. She saw his eyes heavy with grief. She kissed him on the head as a silent reassurance that everything would be all right.

"What happened to Kanak?" she asked.

"He's no longer with us. He left."

"Why?"

"He's bitter toward me."

"He left us? What if something happens to him? He is one of us, he is your brother! You must look for him. You can't let him die!"

"I must let go of the past even though it's hard to forget about my family. My parents are dead, and I haven't seen any of my siblings in many seasons. I haven't heard from the ones who left home or the two who remained. Anything could have happened to them."

Arnaaluk whimpered. "Those terrible tall figures could have killed them!"

Tulok nodded his head numbly. "Yes, I know."

"They will kill anything that moves! I know they are near every time I hear those loud 'bang' noises."

Tulok agreed, "I know what they are capable of doing to us. I also fear those strange creatures with teeth, the creatures that grab you by the paw, and those creatures that hang in between trees and catch you by the neck."

Arnaaluk sighed. "The killers! They don't want us living here!"

"They want us dead because they want the caribou for themselves. We can hide from them, but we also have the power to fight them…but not the courage. Killing one of them will bring death to hundreds of us."

Tulok, nonetheless was also aware of another looming threat. He was aware of a silent and invisible killer. Starvation.

There was a time in the distant past, generations ago, before the killers arrived in the valley of the Yukon River when gunshots were never heard and when wolf families were abundant and intact. Family ties were strong, long-standing hunting strategies were forged, and wolves lived for many years. Many generations ago, these wolves were occasionally stalked by hunters with spears, but the arrival of the tall figures brought an unprecedented onslaught of disease, poisoning, and killing. Everything changed after they disrupted the balance of nature.

Tulok never lived in a time when this land was an unspoiled wilderness. The present world was the only world he knew - a world of traps, poison, guns, and premature death, but he knew of the past through stories from his father, passed down through generations.

Chapter Thirty-Five

The Threat of Starvation

For days, Tulok trekked miles of forests, mountains, and valleys, but he could not find the slightest trace of caribou. He paused in the middle of a forest not far from the den to find a single snowshoe hare. It was not enough to satisfy Arnaaluk's hunger, but anything would help. Arnaaluk was hungry for anything he could catch, sometimes a snowshoe hare, sometimes a ptarmigan.

Tulok returned to the den with the hare in his mouth. Arnaaluk emerged from the entrance to the den and snatched it from him.

Tulok sighed and rested outside. He had been through times of starvation before, especially in late winter when caribou were scarce. He had watched several of his siblings die of starvation. This was a crucial time because Kanak had left and there was just Arnaaluk, Lusa, Kiviaq, and Nova to help him hunt prey.

Late that afternoon, Tulok found a large herd of caribou. He set his sight on a straggling caribou at the back of the herd and raced toward it. During the chase, he made a sudden turn, and the caribou ran farther to the right, separating itself from the others. With the caribou isolated, the wolves cornered it to prevent it from escaping. Tulok from the front, Kiviaq from the left, Lusa from the back, and Nova from the right.

The caribou turned its head left toward Kiviaq, raising its front hooves and charging. It thrust its antlers into Kiviaq's back and side, trampling him and knocking him out of the way. With the circle surrounding the caribou broken, Tulok tried to catch its throat, but nearly got trampled. The caribou fled from the wolves and rejoined the herd.

Tulok approached Kiviaq as he lay writhing on the ground. He took one last look at the herd as they disappeared behind the mountain ahead. It was a terrible failure for him, and his heart ached. He growled and moaned, turning to look at the other wolves. They all trembled, weakened with hunger. Their eyes were sullen. One failure had dampened their spirits and filled them with fear - fear of starvation. Tulok knew there were few caribou herds migrating north. The larger herds were still south and not coming this way any time soon. Would they come back too late?

Tulok returned to the den and spent the evening resting. The wolves, famished and aching from hunger, rested wearily by the den. Tulok felt pain in his shoulder and the pangs of hunger gnawed his belly. Drained of hope and wallowing in frustration, he sighed, unable to rise, sore and strained.

A heavy wet cough awoke Tulok from his sleep. He jumped and rushed toward Kiviaq who was writhing in anguish, starvation aggravating his injuries. Tulok stood over him and looked at Kiviaq's gaunt body. His condition had worsened. The airways in his lungs were clogged with mucus and blood, and he trembled with chills.

Tulok licked him on the side of the face to keep him calm. "Don't worry, Kiviaq, I'm here to help you," he whispered.

Laying by his side, Tulok felt every breath Kiviaq took. His breaths were becoming shorter, painful, and more difficult.

Deep concern overwhelmed Tulok. By now, he knew the inevitable. Kiviaq would not survive. Tulok nudged him, urging him to awaken, but he did not. He had descended into the deep sleep from which he would never return. He took his last breath and faded into eternity.

Tulok stood over Kiviaq's body in grief. He turned his head toward Nova and stood silent for a moment, then let out a dreary howl for Kiviaq, and Lusa and Nova joined him.

Arnaaluk was alone in her den when the bad news came. She listened to the howls of the three wolves and by the tone of their howls, she knew there had been a loss. She listened to each of their voices: the voices of Tulok, Lusa, and Nova, but Kiviaq's howl was not among them.

Arnaaluk instinctively knew of Kiviaq's fate, and she, too, howled in sadness. Collapsing to the floor of her den, she remembered their growing up together, the times they played, and when they mourned for her mother and father. Now, with Kiviaq gone, she realized that she had lost one of her closest friends. She would never forget him.

Chapter Thirty-Six

Hoofbeats of Hope

While the other wolves rested by the den, Nova stayed by his dead brother's side, overcome with grief. He occasionally left to hunt for food, but each time was a long, grueling and fruitless journey. With each step, he grew weaker.

Nova watched for Tulok, hoping he would return with the leg or flank of a caribou. Every time Tulok returned to the den with an empty mouth, Nova grew more discouraged. When Tulok left the den site, Nova would listen for a howl from Tulok, summoning the other wolves to a caribou hunt, but instead of a howl, there was nothing but silence. With no food, Nova's legs wobbled and he lost strength. The death of his brother had weakened his spirit.

Before long, Nova collapsed on his side. He was racked with physical and emotional pain, and much time had passed since he'd eaten. His suffering grew worse and on his last day, Nova's legs were weak and his body gaunt. He trudged through the snow to see his brother's shriveled body for the last time. Nova knew his life was over. He looked over the horizon where storm clouds gathered. The wind picked up and torrents of snow fell from the sky which made it difficult for him to stand or walk.

In the midst of the heavy snow, Nova took one last look at the den. He saw his family waiting for him, but none ran to greet him. They were all famished and grieved over the loss of

Kiviaq. Nova tried to howl with them, but his ribs ached. Collapsing, he tried to pick himself up, but it was no use.

Finally, Nova grew so weak that he struggled to stay alive. The last thought in his mind was *Arnaaluk still lives*, but he had no hope for her or the others in his family. It was better for him to die now, than to face the heartbreaking grief of losing his sister, his aunt, or Tulok. Soon, he lost consciousness, but he no longer felt any pain.

Still grieving over the loss of Kiviaq, Arnaaluk languished in her den. While recovering from the shock of one loss, there came more bad news and more howls of mourning. Arnaaluk managed to pick herself up and look outside to see Nova lying on the ground. She crawled out of the den and ran toward him.

She pawed at his throat and chest, sniffing and nudging him. "Nova! Please wake up! Please!"

She looked at the other two wolves, Lusa and Tulok. They were still breathing, but weak and gaunt, deteriorating from hunger.

Arnaaluk rushed toward Tulok, looking him in the eyes. His expression was gloomier than ever. She nudged him. "Please Tulok! We must find something to eat."

"No, it's no use," he wheezed.

A noise caught Arnaaluk's attention. "What? What was that?" she whispered.

What was that sound? Caribou hooves? The sound of caribou hooves grasped her attention. The caribou herds were passing the hills on the other side of the river. Could this be it? Could the herds finally be migrating to the north? She heard it, but Tulok did not.

"Tulok!" she exclaimed, "I hear caribou! Please! You must..."

"No!" Tulok interrupted, "You're just imagining things."

The rhythm of caribou hooves finally caught Tulok's attention, but he was not encouraged. "It's no use," said Tulok, "Those caribou will probably escape. I don't know if I'm strong enough to catch one."

Arnaaluk nudged him, "Stop being stubborn!" she snapped, "I'm in charge here!" She grabbed him by the shoulder with her teeth. "Listen, Tulok, you will either stay here and die of starvation, or you will die trying."

Tulok wobbled to his feet. He turned to the direction of the herd, inhaling their scent. He crossed the river on the ice, then gathering his strength, he dashed over the hill on the other side.

As Tulok's thin legs crossed the nearby hill, he felt no more hunger, no more pain. The aching in his belly disappeared as his heart rate increased. His mind and body gained strength. Now he was willing to chase a caribou, his will to survive had returned.

Tulok followed the caribou scent to the hills in the northwest. With the scent growing stronger, he picked up his pace, crossing one hill after another. By the time he reached the summit of the last hill, the scent vanished.

Unwilling to accept defeat, Tulok slid downhill. Reaching the foot of the hill, he paused to catch his breath, and sniffed the air. Still no caribou.

Tulok, again, was ready to give up and he was tempted to return to the den, but to turn around and return would mean unavoidable death. Arnaaluk was right. It would be better to die trying than not try at all.

Caribou or no caribou, he pressed on. He continued to the northwest, seeking out the herd that had just passed. Crossing each hill, he paused to sniff the air. Fear of starvation and concern for Arnaaluk's unborn offspring overwhelmed him. Failure would deny them a chance to be born into this world.

Tulok trotted farther north until he reached the bend of the Yukon River. Then, came a familiar scent and the realization burst into his mind, caribou!

He crossed into unknown territory, possibly the territory of other wolves. He did not know, neither did he care. The scent grew stronger with each step, and as he paused to rest, he found he had reached the great mountains to the north.

Tulok's legs trembled with weakness. The temptation to collapse in the snow became great, but he climbed the mountain and stood on the summit, gazing into the valley before him. There, out in a clearing, he found a young caribou trudging through the deep snow. It had been separated from the herd.

Chapter Thirty-Seven

The Wolverine

As Tulok began the chase, the young caribou lagged far behind the others. It stumbled over a rock and broke one of his front legs. The young bull limped through the snow, trying to catch up with the herd. Licking his teeth, Tulok panted as he studied the caribou.

The caribou picked up speed, trying to escape on three legs. As soon as Tulok reached the back legs, he nipped at them. He took a kick to the neck, another to the mouth, and a third to the shoulder, but he was not deterred.

Tulok jumped forward and sank his teeth into the caribou's upper leg. He endured more kicks to the neck, but made another bite to the flank, latching on as hard as he could.

Tulok lost his grip with another kick. He collapsed in the snow with exhaustion and pain, panting and almost unconscious. His mind was fuzzy. He bled from the open wounds on his mouth, coughing up a back tooth and a few drops of blood into the snow. Opening his eyes and licking the blood from his gums and teeth, Tulok followed a trail of blood until he found the young caribou. The caribou, weak from blood loss, toppled, landing in the snow with a thud. Tulok gave the caribou one bite in the throat, clamping his jaws until there was no more breath. He dropped the caribou's head on the ground. Exhausted, he rested next to the lifeless carcass.

After a brief rest, Tulok got back on his feet and prepared to eat. Suddenly, a creature appeared, smaller in size, but fearless and tenacious. A wolverine! A creature with sharp teeth and claws that could fight like a bear and could kill an animal as large as a moose.

The wolverine approached the carcass and grabbed a bite of it. Tulok growled, but the wolverine snarled and prepared to fight. It pounced on Tulok, biting into his shoulder. Tulok flipped the wolverine over and pinned it on the ground, but the wolverine wiggled free. It wrapped itself around Tulok's head and its legs around his neck, latching on to him, trying to suffocate him. It mauled the side of Tulok's lip.

Tulok managed to shake the wolverine off his face, but the wolverine jumped back on him, mauling his other shoulder. Both wolf and wolverine alike rolled through the snow in a chaotic frenzy. The wolverine's claws slashed Tulok's flesh. It seized Tulok's face again, leaving more bite marks and pulled on his muzzle with its jaws. The wolverine crawled on Tulok's back and gave him a powerful bite, almost strong enough to snap his backbone in half. Tulok rolled over, trying to crush it, but the agile creature ran out from under him, sinking its claws into his shoulders and mauling Tulok on his face and neck.

After he had endured multiple bites and ceaseless mauling, Tulok turned and fled from the wolverine. He took one last look as it stood over the stolen carcass.

Tulok collapsed in the snow, his spirit crushed. All hope seemed lost, and death was now inevitable for Arnaaluk and whatever remained of her family. Her offspring would never see the light of day. These thoughts ran through Tulok's mind. To make matters worse, the rest of the caribou herd seemed too far away. The thought of his mate and her unborn pups dying was unbearable.

Chapter Thirty-Eight

A Caribou's Sacrifice

Not admitting defeat, Tulok clung to hope. He could not return to the den without food, so he had to stay with the caribou and take one down. He slowly picked himself up and looked to the north, examining the tracks scattered through the snow. He continued farther north in pursuit of the herd, and then, as if by chance, another caribou appeared. This time, it was an old bull - not a healthy old bull, but weak and arthritic.

Tulok dashed toward it. Once he was close enough, the old bull kicked him in the neck, which stunned Tulok, knocking him to the ground. He struggled in the snow with a bleeding gash on his neck. His spirit, nonetheless, was still strong and in spite of the temptation to give up, he got back on his feet and continued the chase.

Tulok pounced and grabbed the bull's flank with his jaws. The caribou bucked until it shook itself free, but the bite left a deep gash. Tulok was encouraged, springing forward a second time and latching onto the perineum with his strong teeth.

The caribou collapsed and was still for a moment. Then, he jumped back to his feet and tried to shake himself free, but Tulok fastened his jaws shut. In spite of the trauma, the caribou tried to run, as blood poured from his back leg. Finally, the caribou collapsed in the snow and Tulok ran to its front end.

Seeing the caribou alone and helpless, Tulok licked the blood and caribou fur from his gums. The caribou could not rise and defend itself as Tulok stood over its body, panting to catch his breath. He felt encouraged. Before he took the fatal bite, he stopped to think about his mate and her unborn pups, the fate that could befall Arnaaluk if he failed. He could picture her dying from hunger, suffering the same fate as her brothers.

Finally, he took the fatal bite, his teeth piercing through the hide and crushing the throat. He did it! Watching the caribou take its last gasp, he placed his paws on the caribou's side, then picked up the neck and began to drag it back to the den. He was exhausted from his journey, but adrenaline gave him extra strength. After a long journey down the east bank of the river, he arrived at the den. Tulok approached Arnaaluk with the caribou's neck in his mouth.

Arnaaluk crawled out of the den to see Tulok exhausted and bloody, dragging the caribou. She jumped on the carcass and ripped off chunks of fur with Tulok and Lusa joining her. The three wolves devoured everything, stripping the caribou down to the bone, and soon, nothing remained.

Now they relaxed. Arnaaluk crawled back into the den as Tulok and Lusa sat by the entrance. With their bellies swollen with venison, they closed their eyes and drifted off to sleep.

Chapter Thirty-Nine

The Trap

The three wolves rested by the den. Although satisfied from their recent kill, they continued to howl and mourn for Kiviaq and Nova. It was now late April and the weather was chilly, although some of the snow had melted revealing grass underneath. The sun shone warm rays across the river. With more daylight and cloudless skies, there was time to bask in the sun's warmth.

Arnaaluk slept in her den, but occasionally opened her eyes to take in the scent of caribou or other animals that were near. For a time, a beam of light entered the den, illuminating the interior with its bright light. With the passage of time, the beam slowly faded and the den grew dark once again.

Her joints aching from being inside the den, Arnaaluk crawled out and wandered down to the river. She lapped to quench her thirst, then waded and splashed. She broke off chunks of thawing ice and shattered them against rocks.

Tulok listened to the thunder of huge chunks of ice breaking away in the river, then floating downstream. Still sore from fighting the wolverine and tracking caribou, he crawled onto the fresh grass above the den and rolled in it. Once the ice had disappeared, flocks of Canada geese descended on the waters, filling the riverbanks. The entire day had been peaceful. There were no gunshots, no starvation, and no troublesome brother for him to deal with. He gazed at the sun as it slowly disappeared behind the hills west of the river.

At twilight, Tulok pointed his ears, listening for the howls of neighboring wolves. A different scent reached his nose, followed by footsteps in the forest not far away. He expected to find tall figures with large sticks approaching the den and cautiously watched the landscape. There were a few squeaks and a click. These sounds were unfamiliar to Tulok, and for a time, he scanned the nearby woods for signs of danger. In a few moments, the footsteps and scent grew faint and disappeared. For now, the danger had passed, and Tulok closed his eyes, drifting off to sleep.

The following morning, Arnaaluk, still hungry, left the den to search for food. Tulok stayed by the den while Lusa was out tracking caribou. Dark clouds covered the sky and a patchy drizzle watered the ground, turning the snow to ice. Arnaaluk inhaled the scent of the fresh rain and spruce, and the forest floor felt cool and damp.

As she plowed her nose through the brush and sticks on the ground, strong teeth suddenly emerged, snapping around her muzzle. She tried to open her mouth but could not! She pulled on the object, but a strong chain kept it anchored and the teeth on the trap were sharp and powerful. They pierced through the skin on her muzzle and lower jaw, leaving Arnaaluk in agony. Unable to open or escape the trap, she whimpered for help.

Arnaaluk had never seen one of these before! She had heard tales of strong teeth snatching up from the ground and catching a hapless wolf by the paw, and of wolves caught by these

169

objects never being seen again. Sometimes they would be trapped for days. She heard of others who chewed their legs off out of desperation and sometimes bled to death, and those who lost teeth trying to chew through the trap. They would live for a time without food, but then starve.

Tulok heard the snap out in the forest, the same sound he'd heard before his mother died. Fearing something terrible had happened, he rushed into the forest, fearing the worst. To his horror, he discovered Arnaaluk trapped. Her muzzle was caught on something. With dread, Tulok investigated and found it to be the same device that had killed his mother. He grabbed it with his teeth and pulled, but the object was too strong to break and he risked wearing out the teeth he needed to hunt and survive. He could not afford to lose them.

Tulok dropped the object. He tugged on the chain but could not pry it from the ground. Licking the side of Arnaaluk's neck, he tried to keep her calm and then raised his head and howled for help.

Another wolf appeared. Out of desperation, Tulok rushed toward it and found it was Kanak.

"Kanak! Please help her!" Tulok cried.

Kanak froze in his tracks and gazed upon the strange object. "I've never seen one of these before. What is it?"

"It's some strange type of creature with strong teeth," Tulok replied. "I've seen these! They're very hard to escape."

Kanak tried to pry the trap away with his teeth, but Tulok nudged him away, "Should we touch it?"

"Why not?" asked Kanak, "Don't you want me to save her?"

"Yes! Please try!" Backing away from Kanak to give him room, Tulok himself stepped on something cold and hard, and another pair of teeth snapped from the ground, catching his front paw! The teeth poked into his flesh.

"Here's a very interesting situation!" Kanak uttered, seeing the trap caught on Tulok's paw. He turned around and began to trot away.

Tulok snarled at him. "Kanak! What are you doing? You're supposed to help us!"

"Why?" asked Kanak, "You're not my problem."

"If Arnaaluk stays here, she will die!" Tulok snapped, "This is the same thing our mother was caught in!"

Guilt flooded over Kanak and he turned around. He looked at the trap lodged on Arnaaluk's muzzle and began chewing it. As he chewed, his teeth weakened. The hard steel in the trap brought intense pain to his mouth, but he bit harder on the object, bending the steel and biting a hole in its side. A tooth dislodged from his gums and slid down his throat. Kanak choked on the tooth and quickly spat it on the icy ground.

Kanak panted drops of blood, but then turned back to Arnaaluk. He continued gnawing on the trap, widening the holes he had made. More of his teeth became loose and his jaws quickly fatigued. He paused to pant and rest while staring at the holes in the trap.

Assuming the holes were deep enough, he nudged Arnaaluk to encourage her. "Pull on the trap! Do it!"

Arnaaluk pulled as hard as she could, and the steel on the trap bent out of shape. However, it was not enough.

"Come on!" cried Kanak, "You must pull yourself free!"

Kanak grabbed the trap with his teeth, biting harder, trying to soften the steel. He nudged her again, "Don't stop! Keep pulling!"

She pulled again and the trap broke at last, freeing her! She quickly ran to Tulok, whimpering, and started chewing on his trap.

"No, Arnaaluk! Run to the den! You must not be here!" exclaimed Tulok.

"We must save you!" she shrieked.

"You must go back," Tulok groaned, "Go now! Think of our pups!"

Kanak followed her as she fled back to the den.

He turned to look at his brother for the last time. "Tulok, you've had such a wonderful life. I don't see why I should save you. You stole Arnaaluk from me and left me without a family."

"What?" Tulok exclaimed.

"You'll stay there until you die! I'm sorry it has to end this way, Tulok."

Tulok was livid. "Kanak! Come back here! How could you do this to your own brother?"

Chapter Forty

Kanak's Sacrifice

Kanak returned to the den with Arnaaluk. He nuzzled her on the side of the neck.

Arnaaluk snarled and snapped at him. "How could you leave your brother out there?"

"He doesn't have a chance!" Kanak replied, "I can't save him."

Arnaaluk stood before him, her tail straight back. "You're lying!"

She nipped him on the shoulder. "Please! Go and free him!"

Kanak growled at her in defiance. "No! I won't! I've come back for what's mine!" He nipped her on her side and she let out a yelp of pain.

Arnaaluk circled Kanak, scowling at him with the fur on her back raised and her lips curled.

Realizing he'd made her angry, Kanak cowered before Arnaaluk. She jumped on him, mauling him on his shoulders and chest. She grabbed him by the neck and dragged him to the edge of the forest.

She stood over him, growling in his face. "You *will* save Tulok! You *will* rescue him! He's my mate! I belong to him and he belongs to me, and I'm never going to accept you." She placed her teeth near the veins in Kanak's neck. "Save him, or I swear, I will kill you!"

Kanak panted with shock. "Arnaaluk!" he whimpered, "You mean you've accepted him?"

"It's true! And we will raise a family together!"

"No! How could you do this to me? How could you reject me! I'll do anything I can for you! Please!"

"You'll do anything for me?"

"Yes! Anything! I'll do anything you want me to do! Just tell me!"

"Free your brother!"

"Yes! I'll do it!"

Kanak rushed back into the forest to find Tulok. Kanak, hesitant to save him, stood by him in indecision.

"Please, help me!" Tulok groaned.

"Yes! I...am here to help you. Or maybe I won't. Why should I save you? You've never done anything for me."

Kanak turned and tried to walk away, but as he stepped, steel jaws snapped around his front paw! He struggled and howled for help.

"Now...we are even," Tulok growled.

Kanak paused. He sat next to his brother, haunted by the thought of losing Arnaaluk to him. He tried to gnaw the trap on his own paw, but his conscience pricked him. Kanak thought of Arnaaluk's pups and how they would need a father, and what Tulok told him about their mother's death. Kanak could not bear the thought of losing his own brother. Tulok was still family to him.

Kanak looked at Tulok, trapped beside him. Kanak was truly sorry for the way he had treated him. He turned to the trap on his brother's paw and took a deep bite at it. He pressed hard with his teeth until he created a deep cut along the trap's upper jaw. Gnawing until the teeth on the left side of his mouth were loosening, Kanak kept biting and chewing the trap until it was almost severed. His teeth were broken and blood streamed from his mouth.

Kanak nudged Tulok, trying to persuade him to pull on the trap. "Do it! Free yourself!"

Tulok was skeptical. "It's no use!"

Kanak nudged him again. "Do it! I already saved Arnaaluk and I'll save you, too."

Tulok pulled as hard as he could, bending the trap out of shape until it broke. He was finally free.

Kanak nudged him away. "Now is your chance! Go!"

Tulok refused to leave his brother's side. "Why did you save me? Why didn't you save yourself?"

He tried to chew the trap off Kanak's paw, but Kanak nipped at him. "Please leave!" he snarled.

"I must save you! I can't leave you here to die!"

"Tulok! You cannot chew this trap and break your teeth! You need those teeth to help Arnaaluk and your family survive! You are my brother! You were worth saving. There may be no one else left in our family."

Tulok tried to bend the trap with his teeth, but Kanak kept nipping at him. "Go!" barked Kanak, "They will be here any moment!"

"I can't leave you!" Tulok pleaded.

Kanak gave Tulok one last lick on the cheek. "Go! Leave me alone!"

Tulok laid his head on Kanak's neck. "Please, Kanak!" he whimpered, "Let me free you! Please come home with me! We can make things right between us."

"No! Just leave me! Go and raise a family, Tulok! I will save myself if I can."

Tulok stood by Kanak, gazing into the eyes of his brother. "I'm sorry, brother," he whispered. He rubbed his head against Kanak's neck, then limped away and disappeared. He did not return to the den but remained in the forest watching Kanak, hiding among the trees. The temptation to free his brother was great, but he could not go back. Kanak was right. The trapper could be there at any moment.

Kanak pulled on the trap with his jaws. He gnawed on it, putting more strain on his teeth. They fell out one by one until there were none left and his mouth was soaked with blood.

Even if he escaped the trap, he could not survive much longer. Without his teeth, he would be unable to catch food and eat. He remained in the trap all day and into the night.

Another day passed. As Kanak sat awaiting his imminent doom, his ears were ringing and everything was silent. There was no wind, not even a breeze. It was so quiet that Kanak could feel and hear his heart pounding. Then, Kanak smelled someone approaching. The scent was followed by the sound of footsteps – the snapping of twigs on the forest floor and the crunching of icy snow. Kanak shivered with fear, his stomach fluttered and his legs and body shook. All hope was lost. He struggled violently, but the teeth of the trap sheared off his fur and cut into his skin. His paw was swollen and numb and a stream of blood drained from the deep cut on his leg, forming a puddle beneath him. Trying to wrench his paw back and forth to break the carpal bones and free himself, Kanak realized it was too late.

The tall figure arrived at the trap, casting a shadow over him. Kanak howled in terror repeatedly, but there was no one to save him. He heard a loud click in the trees next to him. He fell silent and lowered his head, gazing with a sad face at the tall figure, pleading silently with him.

A moment of silence passed. Bang! A fatal blast vibrated through the air and echoed through the forests and hills. A hot bullet entered Kanak's chest, piercing his liver. A few more moments of silence passed, and a second click was heard. Bang!

Chapter Forty-One

The Loss of a Brother

When the sound of gunshot reached Tulok's ears, he froze among the safety of the trees, hesitant to approach the traps. When he heard footsteps walking away, he crept forward. Sensing no more danger, he rushed toward the site of the traps.

Tulok sniffed the gunpowder permeating the air as he rushed toward the ghastly scene. Nothing remained of Kanak except blood spattered across the thawing snow and fragments of his dark gray fur. A trail of oval-shaped tracks marked the icy snow and mud.

Tulok hung his head low, slinking back to the den along the river. When he came within sight of Lusa, he gazed mournfully into her eyes. The two wolves broke out into a somber howl. The howl meant only one thing - Kanak was gone forever.

During the day and into the evening, Tulok sat by the den with a paw over his eyes. Every passing moment seemed like an eternity as he grieved for his brother and the awful fate he had met. Tulok was lost in the memories of Kanak - their fights, the enmity between them, and the peace they made at the end. Then it all came to an end as Kanak died alone.

An entire season of grief and mourning passed. Arnaaluk sat in her den, shocked by Kanak's violent death. Tulok's sorrowful howls filled her heart with sadness and she raised her head and howled, too, in an eerie, but beautiful voice. She realized how much Tulok had loved his brother and how much he had loved his family.

Arnaaluk's growling stomach kept her awake much of the time. She frequently left the den to search for food. She would consume twenty or thirty voles and gorged herself on the carcasses of the caribou Tulok killed. In time, Arnaaluk no longer felt hungry, as her body was satisfied and her belly was full and swollen. All she could do was sleep. She dreamed of being with her two brothers once again, fighting and playing, a dream that kept playing in her head. Sometimes, though, she slept peacefully and did not feel the cold wind or hear the rain outside.

One evening, Arnaaluk awoke to the unborn pups moving inside her womb. She rolled over on her back, then stretched her legs and poked her head above the entrance to the den. She did not see Tulok outside.

"Where's Tulok?" she asked Lusa.

"I think he's out hunting for food."

Arnaaluk found Tulok deep in the forest, resting on the spot where Kanak met his untimely end. All that remained of Kanak were pieces of fur. Arnaaluk approached Tulok and rubbed her head against his neck, lying next to him.

"I can't believe I let him die," Tulok said sadly. "I could have saved him."

"There wasn't anything you could've done to save him. Kanak did something very heroic for you. You should be thankful."

"I am thankful," said Tulok.

"He was your brother. You may have been rivals, but you and Kanak were still family."

Arnaaluk lay quietly, remembering what she had learned over the past winter. She had learned the true nature of the wolf, and now had learned loyalty through Kanak's selfless act. Through the difficult circumstances she had faced, she learned the lessons of love and devotion to her family.

More days passed. Tulok sniffed a piece of Kanak's fur and touched it with his paw. Now Tulok held the last remaining sign of Kanak as he trembled with grief. The wind picked up, making the temptation to release the piece of fur stronger. Tulok realized it was time to let go of the past, and with sadness, he lifted his paw from the ground. The last piece of fur slipped away from him, floated through the trees and mingled with the loose snow. By this time, the rain, snow and wind had cleaned the last traces of blood and tracks from the scene. Every trace of Kanak disappeared forever. Tulok padded back to the den and sat outside, remaining there for the rest of the afternoon and into the evening.

High-pitched whimpering sounds coming from inside the den interrupted Tulok's grief. Lifting his head, he trotted up the short slope to the entrance. Tulok paused and took a deep breath, then peered inside. Arnaaluk sat before him with four newborn pups crawling on the ground next to her. He watched as she prepared to nurse them, nudging each of the pups toward her warm underbelly. Tulok panted with joy, then he and Lusa howled, proclaiming the birth of this litter.

Chapter Forty-Two

A New Normal

The winter was gone and it was almost summer. Bright green grass consumed the landscape and most of the snow had disappeared. Wildflowers bloomed in the valleys and along the banks of the river. Arnaaluk stood by the clearing, teaching one of her pups to howl. She howled first, then watched as the pup howled back in response. Lusa was sitting by the den, exhausted from the time she spent helping Arnaaluk care for the pups. Two of the pups played, one chewing on Tulok's tail, the other crawling on his back. Tulok, although sometimes abrasive and testy, didn't mind the pups crawling upon him. He sat watching the sky and land, guarding the pups from predators such as an eagle, bear, or a wolverine.

As sunset turned to twilight, Arnaaluk put the pups to rest and approached Tulok, snuggling next to him. It was their first chance to spend time together in over a season. While she was not paying attention, one of her pups wandered down the hillside not far from the den. As the young pup crawled through the grass, a hand suddenly reached down and grabbed it by the neck.

Arnaaluk soon noticed one of her pups was missing and a dreaded scent reached her nostrils. Running downhill to the edge of the nearby forest, she found a tall figure walking away. She sniffed the ground to find the scent of her own pup in the grass. Furtively following the tall figure as it approached a tent deep in the woods, Arnaaluk saw the man holding her pup by the scruff of its neck, as he crawled inside.

Arnaaluk paced outside the tent, howling for her pup. The man emerged from the entrance and tried to shoo her away. Arnaaluk backed away a few steps and stood in front of him, but did not attack.

She could hear her pup whimpering inside the tent and howled for him, but the man did not respond. Once again, a hand protruded from the entrance shooing at her, and she retreated into the woods. Arnaaluk watched the tent from a distance, but she didn't dare approach again.

Finally, after she waited for some time, the man left the tent and walked away. Arnaaluk cautiously approached, crawled inside, and found her pup in a small hard box. She nudged it with her paws, tipped it over and began chewing on the door of the box, pulling it with her jaws. Unable to open it, she dragged it far outside the tent and took it deep into the forest. She grabbed the latch with her teeth, bending it until it snapped free and the door swung open. Arnaaluk stuck her head inside, picked up her pup by the scruff of his neck, and raced back to her den. The sight of a man in this area filled her with dread. This area was no longer safe for them.

As Tulok sat by the river, he was overwhelmed with concern. His family was no longer safe from hunters, he smelled their scent more often now. Then, another thought crossed his mind. *What had become of his family? Are any of them still alive?* He had a strong desire to reconnect with them, especially following the death of Kanak.

Tulok left Arnaaluk, Lusa, and the pups for the rest of the night. He traveled into the mountains to the north and arrived where his family once lived. No wolf stood there to greet him.

Tulok gazed upon the land where he was born. He howled, but there was no response. Again he howled, and again, no answer. He looked at the entrance to the den where he was born, but it was overgrown with vegetation and the top had caved in from erosion.

Tulok ascended to the summit of the mountain, howling a third time, but still no response. He looked to the south, to the land where Lycargus and his family once lived, but there was no howl nor a sign of another wolf.

As he approached the northern side of what had once been the territory of Lycargus, he noticed something strange. Closed steel traps and trash littered the ground. Some of the trees had broken snares between them and there were fresh footprints in the mud. Now Tulok understood what had happened. Whoever was left of Lycargus' family was in extreme danger.

Tulok howled for the fourth time, and this time a response came, but the howl didn't come from another wolf in his family. The howl was confrontational. Tulok turned and ran, fearing he might be in the territory of unfriendly wolves.

Once again, Tulok returned to the place where he had saved Arnaaluk from Lycargus. The trees and landscape reminded him of when he first met her. Now Lycargus was gone, but Tulok did not feel happy about his death as he knew this could have happened to himself. His mind flashed back to that fatal gunshot that had claimed the life of the enemy wolf.

Tulok was grateful that he, Lusa, and Arnaaluk survived the winter, but he realized this was no happy ending for many others. Tulok knew Lycargus had a family, too. He had the same hopes, dreams, and will to survive as Tulok.

Tulok howled once again, but this time, there was no response. He lowered his head and sighed, his heart sick with dismay. When he was young, this area had many wolves who controlled the vast populations of caribou, moose, and Dall sheep. Would this be the future? The encroachment of man and the wolves' disappearance?

Tulok knew the structure of the wolf family, how every wolf in a family unit has a role. He knew that wolves were not herd animals, like caribou and moose, and must never be treated as such. These were not just wolves that men killed, they were fathers, mothers, uncles, aunts, daughters and sons. Elimination of one wolf had disastrous consequences. It broke apart entire families and severed relationships, and Tulok's old family was no exception. These men destroyed generations of hunting skills and stifled the crucial role the wolf played keeping nature in balance.

When Tulok returned to the den, he sat next to Arnaaluk, sighed, and closed his eyes. He faded into sleep and dreamed of the howls of his family. The howls were soon mingled with gunshots and the snapping of traps. Then came the images of his two youngest siblings whimpering in pain and hunger, their bodies growing gaunt with starvation. He awoke, tormented by the thought that they possibly had died.

Tulok knew that without the hunting skills of his parents, the younger wolves would be incapable of catching caribou on their own. There was little chance they could have survived through the harsh winters since he had gone. Any hope of him reconnecting with his family had been shattered by the death of Kanak.

Tulok never forgot about Kanak. Kanak's death had left a vacuum in his heart, and for many days after his death, Tulok returned to the spot where Kanak had died. For a time, he whimpered for his siblings. Each time, as he listened to the sounds of the night, the howls of wolves were absent. Other than the rustle of grass and the spruce trees in the night wind, it was silent.

Tulok missed the days when the howls of wolves filled the air. It was clear that humans were encroaching upon wolf habitat and many wolves in the area were either fleeing or dying. Every wolf in this land faced the frailty of life and the inescapable reality of death.

Chapter Forty-Three

An Uncertain Future

One morning, Tulok, Lusa, Arnaaluk and the four pups traveled north along the river in search of a new home. Tulok turned his head toward the den as if to say goodbye and listened to the howl of a wolf not far away. He knew this was the same howl he had heard the night before.

"Whose howl is that?" he asked.

Arnaaluk howled in reply. "I know who it is, he's one of my older brothers! He lives to the north!"

"Is he friendly?" asked Tulok.

"He's as friendly as you are. You've never heard of my extended family, have you?"

"No, I haven't."

At mid-day, the wolves stopped to rest. They made one last somber howl for their losses over the past winter, then they continued their journey throughout the afternoon and into the evening.

As night fell, Tulok and Arnaaluk settled next to each other. A howl from Arnaaluk's brother let them know he was headed in their direction. While waiting for his arrival, they each thought about what lay ahead. The future for them was uncertain, and they did not know how long they could last. They finally closed their eyes and fell asleep.

As if in a dream, Tulok opened his eyes. The wind blew over the mountains and forests, and then mingled with ghostly howls. As Tulok looked to the sky, he could see figures of wolves howling within the Aurora Borealis. He wondered who they could be. Could they be the spirits of his ancestors? Ascending a nearby mountain, he stood on the summit. He recognized the howls of each of them then, he realized they were his brothers and sisters. Tulok stood before these flaming figures, then bade them farewell with a howl. Someday, he would see them again on the other side, at the end of his life's journey.

Once the apparition had vanished, Tulok howled again. A mystery resonated through his howl, causing all who heard to still their thoughts and listen. It was a howl of sadness, demanding understanding, a howl challenging those who heard to reject the myths, tales, hate, and fear, and learn the true nature of the wolf.

Tulok descended the mountain. He looked one last time to watch the Aurora Borealis flashing over him, and dissolve into the night sky.

Did You Enjoy This Book?

Your feedback will help the author provide the best quality books and help other readers discover this book.

If you would take a few minutes of your time to share your thoughts about this work, it would not only be beneficial to the author, but to other readers as well. You can leave a review on the retailer of your choice and/or send the author an email at brett.roehr@gmail.com with your honest feedback.

Thank you so much for reading. A portion of sales from the purchase of this book will support the International Wolf Center, Living with Wolves and the Wolf Conservation Center, which will allow them to continue their work supporting and advocating for North America's wolves.

Made in United States
Troutdale, OR
10/29/2024

24102949R00127